JACK HIGGINS
WITH JUSTIN RICHARDS
FIRST STRIKE

First published in paperback in Great Britain by HarperCollins *Children's Books* 2009
HarperCollins *Children's Books* is a division of HarperCollins*Publishers* Ltd
77-85 Fulham Palace Road, Hammersmith, London W6 8JB

Visit us on the web at
www.harpercollins.co.uk

2

Text copyright © Harry Patterson 2009

ISBN 978-0-00-730048-8

Harry Patterson reserves the right to be identified as the author of the work.

Printed and bound in England by Clays Ltd, St Ives plc

Other titles by Jack Higgins with Justin Richards:

Sharp Shot
Death Run
Sure Fire

About the authors:

Jack Higgins lived in Belfast till the age of twelve. Leaving school at fifteen, he spent three years with the Royal Horse Guards, serving on the East German border during the Cold War. His subsequent employment included occupations as diverse as circus roustabout, truck driver, clerk, teacher and university lecturer. *The Eagle Has Landed* turned him into an international bestselling author, and his novels have since sold over 250 million copies and have been translated into fifty-five languages.

Justin Richards is the is the author of dozens of books, including many *Doctor Who* novels, *The Death Collector* and his *Agent Alfie* series for younger readers. He worked in the computer industry before moving into full-time writing and editing and has also written for the stage and the screen.

Prologue

Rich watched the tanks rolling down the main street. Civilians leaped aside. Children watched wide-eyed from shadowy doorways. Soldiers marched behind the tanks, grim-faced and determined.

These images were repeated on television screens all round the restaurant. The grim news reports they showed were a stark contrast to the upbeat 1980s dance track that was throbbing through the place. A teenage waitress on roller skates with a red and white striped uniform and braces on her teeth spun to a perfect stop beside Jade and Rich. She smiled at their dad.

"Can I get you guys some drinks?"

In the US-themed restaurant, its walls adorned with road signs and music posters from the 1950s, her West

Country accent was out of place. Up till then, Rich could have forgotten that he was in England.

"You're driving," Jade warned her dad before he could order. "I'll have a sparkling mineral water."

"Milkshake," Rich decided. "Chocolate fudge."

"That is *so* bad for you," Jade told him.

But Rich just grinned. His twin sister could be such a health freak. "I know."

"What draught beer do you have?" John Chance asked.

The waitress started to list American beers.

Jade glared at her dad. "I *said*, you're driving."

"Just curious. I'll have a pineapple juice," he said. "With ice. If I'm allowed."

"Ice is OK," Jade confirmed.

"Made from frozen vodka if you can manage it," Chance added. He grinned. "Kidding," he assured the waitress.

"Right. I'll be straight back with your drinks, and I'll take your food order then. OK?" She didn't wait for a reply.

On the TV screens a reporter was talking, though the sound was muted. Text flashed up underneath him: *Chinese Peacekeepers enter Wiengwei province... No sign of missing US air crew... Chinese deny airmen have been arrested...*

8

"I don't know why they do that," said Jade.

"They're worried the rebels are getting more support," said Rich.

"The Chinese have had trouble in Wiengwei ever since they invaded back in 1950," Chance added. "At the time the western world was more concerned about Tibet. They hardly noticed what was happening at the same time down the road."

"I *meant*," said Jade, "why do they show the news channel with the sound turned down and music blaring out? I mean – what's the point? You have to guess what's happening. It's just like visual noise and a confusing tickertape."

...White House accused of abandoning airmen... President refuses to condemn Chinese...

"You can sort of see what's going on," said Rich.

The scrolling caption across the bottom of the screen now read: *Still no sign of rebel leader Marshal Wieng.*

"Only because we saw the news before we came out this evening," Jade told him. The 6 o'clock broadcast had been almost entirely devoted to the developing story: an American military plane appeared to have gone down over Chinese airspace, but the Americans were refusing to confirm that their men had even been there, and the Chinese were denying having captured them. "And because we've got Mr Global Trouble-Shooter here to help." She turned to her dad. "I bet you were there in Wiengwei in 1950 when China invaded or annexed it or whatever, weren't you?"

Chance laughed. "How old do you think I am?" He leafed through the large glossy menu. "I have been to Wiengwei, actually" he admitted. "But rather more recently."

"Official visit?" Rich wondered.

"Sort of. Well, no, not exactly. The ribs look good. What are you two having?"

"I'll have a burger," Rich decided.

"Jade?" Chance asked.

But she wasn't listening. Jade was watching the waitress roller-skating across the restaurant carrying a tray with a large bottle of champagne balanced on it.

"Who does that?" she said. "Who comes out on a Friday night to a diner like this and orders champagne? At least you were asking about beer," she told Chance. "If you ordered champagne to go with a burger or ribs, I'd be seriously worried."

"I'd be seriously impressed," said Rich, "if you could

get champagne while Jade's on the case."

The waitress spun to a halt right next to their table.

"Your champagne, sir," she said.

Jade's eyes widened.

Rich's mouth dropped open in awe. "How did you do that?"

Chance seemed every bit as surprised as his children. "I didn't order champagne. I asked for pineapple juice."

The waitress continued to smile, unperturbed. "Your friend ordered it for you." She put the bottle down on the table, together with a glass. Then she handed Chance a folded slip of paper. "He seems a nice man." She leaned closer. "Must be very wealthy!"

Chance took a quick look at the paper. "Appearances can be deceptive." He swung round in his chair, scanning the restaurant.

"Who is it? Who's it from?" Jade asked.

Chance handed her the paper, and she unfolded it. Rich leaned across to read what was written on it. Scrawled in block letters, the message said:
Urgent I speak with you now.

I am in danger, and things are going nuclear!
Only you can stop it.

"But who is it from?" said Rich.

Chance pointed across the restaurant. On the other side of the bar, close to the far window, a man was getting slowly to his feet. He was wearing a smart, pale linen suit. His face was weathered like old stone. He had dark, thinning hair and a neatly-trimmed moustache. The man raised a hand in greeting.

"Ralph!" said Jade.

That wasn't his real name. But it was the name they all knew him by. Ralph was a villain, who ran an organised crime syndicate in Eastern Europe. He had no loyalty except to himself, and Rich knew that he could have them all killed just as soon as buy them champagne, if it suited his purposes.

"What does he want?" Rich wondered.

"I don't know," Chance grimaced. "But I doubt if he's really in as much danger as he'd like us to think."

On the other side of the room, Ralph was smiling. He spread his arms in a generous, welcoming gesture. At that moment the window behind him exploded into fragments as the sound of a gunshot rang out.

A red stain appeared on the front of Ralph's pale jacket. He looked down at it, surprised. Then he fell forwards, crashing down on the table, sending glasses and crockery flying.

Instinctively, Rich and Jade ducked.

Chance was already running. Before the sound of the second shot, he was sprinting towards Ralph's motionless body – colliding with a roller-skating waiter and sending him spinning away. People were scrambling to their feet or throwing themselves to the floor in confusion as the second shot hammered through a table and into the floor.

"Get an ambulance!" Chance shouted as he reached Ralph. He grabbed a handful of paper napkins from the nearest table and balled them into a wad, which he pressed to the red stain on Ralph's shirt. "Ambulance!" he yelled again. "Now."

The waitress who'd brought the champagne kneeled beside Chance and Ralph. Her face was pale.

"Is he...?"

"He's still breathing. But it's not looking good."

Chance grabbed the girl's hand and pushed it down on top of the wad of napkins. "Hold that there, tight as you can, till the paramedics get here."

"Where are you going?"

But Chance was already gone.

Jade kneeled down beside the waitress. "He'll be after the gunman," she explained.

The waitress stared at her, mouth open.

"How's Ralph doing?" Rich asked, joining them. There were people standing round watching now.

"How…" Ralph gasped. His breathing was ragged and noisy. A trickle of blood escaped from the corner of his mouth. "How… do you think… I'm doing?" he gasped. "Is my suit OK?"

His eyelids fluttered, then closed. Ralph sank back into Jade's arms.

The assassin had made a mistake firing twice. The target – Ralph – was already down. The chances were that no one would have seen where the first shot had come from.

But Chance had seen the muzzle flash from the second. It had come from a small, raised wooded area that screened the restaurant car park from the main road beyond. The road was a busy dual-carriageway, so the assassin's only realistic escape route was through the car park. He probably had a car ready.

Chance looked round as he sprinted from the restaurant. There was no sign of a car conveniently waiting. But there was movement in the shrubs along the car-park fence. The vaguest of dark silhouettes fluttered against the evening sky.

Zig-zagging to make himself a harder target, Chance ran for the silhouette. As he moved, he reached inside his jacket. Not because he had a gun, but because he wanted the assassin to think he did.

Ahead of him, a figure in nondescript dark clothing broke cover and pushed its way out of the trees and bushes. The figure was wearing a baseball cap pulled down low, but a long plait of black hair hung down its back.

It was a woman.

The would-be assassin was carrying a rifle with a telescopic sight attached. It looked like an LR153 – accurate up to 600 metres. It was not the ideal weapon to defend herself with, though she swung it up in an arc and loosed off a shot at Chance.

He ignored it. The bullet was travelling faster than sound, and he'd heard the shot without feeling an impact, which meant he hadn't been hit. He was close enough to the woman that she didn't have time to stop and take proper aim. He kept running – in a straight line now, on a course to intercept her as she sprinted down the grassy bank and into the car park.

There was a car in the way, double-parked behind a large people carrier. Chance leaped over the car, sliding across the bonnet and back on his feet in an instant.

But there was no sign of her. The assassin was gone.

Chance kept moving, turning all the time, looking for any movement.

Then he spotted her. She was behind the people carrier, trying to use the large vehicle for cover, but he could make out her vague reflection in the side windows of another car. He smiled. If he couldn't see her properly, then she couldn't see him. He moved stealthily towards the people carrier.

Then suddenly, he was running towards the back of the vehicle. Round the people carrier, and increasing his speed. The woman had her back to him, peering round the front of the vehicle. Chance dropped his shoulder and slammed into the dark-clad shape on the other side, sending her flying.

The rifle skidded away, under another car and out of reach. The woman rolled as she fell and was immediately back on her feet, her hands raised and tensed in a classic karate stance. Her cap had come off, and Chance could see now that she was oriental..

She leaped at him, hands moving rapidly, chopping through the air.

Chance parried the blows and managed to get in a punch of his own. It connected with the assassin's stomach and she doubled up, staggering away. Chance moved forward.

She looked up at him, still bent over in pain. Her face was contorted with hatred and anger. Her eyes, he saw, were different colours – one green and the other blue. He stepped towards her.

The sudden sound of the siren made them both glance away. A police car was turning across the oncoming traffic outside as it sped into the car park, headlights flashing in time with the blue lights on top. An ambulance was close behind it.

In that moment, there was another noise. An engine roared into life and a red Toyota shot out of a parking space nearby. It reversed rapidly, tyres screeching, right at John Chance. As it reversed, the back door swung open.

Chance leaped out of the way as the car skidded to a halt right where he had been standing. Seconds later it was moving again. It swerved round the approaching police car and accelerated past the ambulance out on to the main road.

Inside the car, Chance could clearly see an oriental woman with a long plaited pigtail of black hair.

Jade felt helpless. She stood back to allow the two paramedics to tend to Ralph. One of them replaced the wad of napkins, with gauze and bandages. The other readied a wheeled stretcher and set up a drip.

"This your dad?" one of the paramedics asked.

"No, my dad's chasing the gunman."

The paramedic raised an eyebrow.

Police were moving people back and starting to take statements. Chance pushed his way to the front and spoke quietly but urgently with the policeman in charge. Jade and Rich hurried across to join him.

"And put a guard on the wounded man's hospital room." Chance was saying. "I'll have someone call your superiors with authorisation." He turned to call across to the paramedics: "How is he?"

"Not good," came the reply. "Right, everyone stand back please, stretcher coming through."

"Did you get him?" Rich asked as they watched Ralph being loaded into the ambulance.

Chance shook his head. "*Her*, actually. I got the number of the getaway car, and called it in to Ardman, but they've probably dumped it already."

Ardman was Chance's boss. He ran a secret group of agents that handled missions deemed too sensitive for the main security services. Chance was one of Ardman's senior operatives.

"I hope Ralph's going to be OK," said Jade.

"So do I," Chance agreed. "He wanted to tell us something important. Important enough for someone else to try to kill him. But what was it?"

"And who was the assassin?" said Rich.

His father was staring past him, his attention suddenly fixed on one of the many TV screens. The music had stopped, and above the muted hubbub of conversation, the newsreader's voice was just audible.

"As well as Marshal Wieng, there is also no sign of his second in command, Colonel Shu – who has already been indicted by the international courts for war crimes and crimes against humanity."

The picture on the screen was of an oriental woman with long, jet black hair. One of her eyes was emerald green. The other was sky blue.

1

They sat in the corner of the hospital café. Visiting time was over for the evening and the place was quiet. Even so, John Chance and Hilary Ardman's conversation was barely louder than a whisper.

Rich and Jade listened, but said nothing. Rich was eating biscuits. Jade had an unopened carton of orange juice in front of her. Chance was on his third black coffee and Ardman had a stainless-steel pot of tea that he seemed unimpressed with.

Ardman was holding the note Ralph had sent over to Chance with the champagne. "I'll get this to the forensics people; they might be able to tell us something. Where the paper was made, how long ago it was written, if it's actually Ralph's handwriting. Something."

"We can find all that out, but I'm not sure it will help. What we really need to know what is it *means*," Chance pointed out.

"Yes." Ardman sniffed. "He could have been more helpful."

"He was expecting to speak to me," said Chance.

"So why send the note?" Jade asked. "Why not just come over and chat?"

"Perhaps he felt guilty about what happened last time we met," said Rich.

"Guilty – Ralph?" Chance shook his head. "Yes, I know he set us up against the Mafia, and planted a bomb on you, Rich. But he won't have any regrets about that. His overriding concern is always for himself and how he can turn a profit. So it's more likely the champagne was a peace offering. He wanted to make sure I'd hear him out, not punch him out."

"It was a risk," Ardman said. He opened the lid of his teapot and poked at the teabag inside with a spoon. "He's a wanted man in this country, remember. Oh, he can slip in and out on a false passport easily enough, but making contact with someone who'd recognise him is a big risk. He has no reason to think you'd be friendly towards him. Yet he wanted to tell you something. And not over the phone, but in person."

"And he got shot," Rich added.

"Which suggests whatever he had to say was important." Ardman gave up on the teapot and read the note again. "I don't care for his choice of the word *nuclear*."

"He might not mean it literally," said Chance.

"It's a shame we can't ask him yet."

"How's he doing?" Rich asked. The doctors had been vague when they had spoken to them, but he thought they might have been more open with Ardman.

"Not good," Ardman said. "They've operated, as you know, and removed the bullet from his lung, but he's still in a coma. He may come out of it in the next day or two. Or the next month or so. Or never."

"So the note really is all we have," said Jade.

"Well, we do have a good idea of who the sniper was," Chance pointed out.

"I'd almost rather we didn't." Ardman leaned back in his chair as he considered. "Another false passport job, I suspect. I really must talk to the borders and immigration people about how she got here undetected. But a more pressing question is, why does Colonel Shu, one of the most wanted war criminals in the world, go to the trouble

23

and expense of coming to an out-of-town diner in deepest, darkest Gloucestershire to kill a gentleman – I use the term loosely – who runs one of the most successful crime syndicates in Eastern Europe?"

"And why do it just as the province she's trying to liberate is being invaded by the Chinese?" Rich added.

Ardman frowned. "Not *invaded*, please. It is a Chinese province; they're just asserting their rule."

"Is she working for this Marshal Wieng?" Jade asked.

"Almost certainly," her father told them. "They've fought together since the rebellion really got going in the 1990s. Not that Wiengwei was ever quiet. Marshal Wieng claims to be a direct descendent of the original Emperor Wieng Tso – an equally war-like man who founded the province, and gave his name to it."

"And *is* he a descendent?" asked Rich.

"Doesn't matter," Ardman said. "The point is that the claim has focused the rebels and garnered them more support. Whether it's true or not won't make a difference now. After the Red Army rooted out most of the rebels in 1998, the province has been kept under tight control. But the Chinese took their eye off the ball rather; distracted by earthquakes and Olympics, among other things. That gave Marshal Wieng the opportunity to come out of hiding and start gathering new support."

"Does this Marshal Wieng have nukes?" Rich asked. "Could that be what Ralph meant?"

"The Chinese used to have a couple of strategic missile bases in the province," Ardman said, "but nowhere near the areas where the rebels are active. The bases are still there, but the missiles were withdrawn and decommissioned back in the eighties."

"I guess we just have to hope that Ralph pulls through," said Chance.

"He's a rogue," Ardman said thoughtfully. "But you know I do actually quite like the man."

"Me too," Rich agreed. "Even if he did plant a bomb on me."

"He helped us in Krejikistan," said Jade. "And he was being threatened by the Mafia last time we met, so he didn't have much choice."

They sat in silence for a while. Then Ardman said: "Oh, they found the car, by the way. Abandoned and torched. Not much hope we'll learn anything there." He stood up. "I'd better be getting back to the office. The doctors here know to call me immediately if there's any change and I'll let you know at once. But I expect you'll be in Washington before anything happens."

"It'll give us something to tell the President," Rich joked.

Rich, Jade and their father had been invited to a special reception at the White House. It was a way for the President to thank them for saving his life after some trouble in the Middle East a few weeks previously. Rich had hoped for a medal, but since the whole incident was being kept secret, a White House reception was the next best thing.

"We should be getting back too," said Chance to the twins.

"There's a little shop here," said Jade. "I think I'll take Ralph some flowers before we go."

"He won't see them," Rich told her.

"He will when he wakes up. And he might smell them."

"I'll walk you back to your car," Chance told Ardman. "Meet me at the main entrance," he said to Rich and Jade.

"I'll come with you," Rich told his dad.

"You'll go with Jade."

"Oh right – you're doing secret talk. No kids allowed, I get it."

Chance smiled. "Don't let your sister spend too much on the flowers."

26

*

It seemed miles back to Ralph's private room. Jade and Rich had been allowed only a minute in there before. Just long enough to see that Ralph appeared to be sleeping peacefully. But the constant bleep of a heart monitor and the drips and wires attached to Ralph suggested otherwise.

The plain-clothes police officer sitting outside the door had smiled sympathetically at them when they left. But now his chair was empty.

"I thought he was supposed to be on guard all the time?" said Rich.

Jade had opted for an arrangement that came in its own vase, and had to peer round the enormous bouquet to see what he meant.

"Maybe he's checking on Ralph."

There was a small, round window set high in the door. Rich looked through, and saw that there was someone in the room. A female doctor or nurse in her white coat was checking the monitoring equipment.

"He's not in there."

The flowers brushed against Rich's cheek as Jade joined him at the window.

"He's just nipped off to the loo or to get a coffee or something while the doctor's here."

Jade didn't bother to knock. She just opened the door and walked in.

Rich was right behind her. Jade looked round for somewhere to put down the vase of flowers, but Rich was facing the doctor as she turned. He had barely registered her black hair before, but as she turned he saw the slight bulge under the back of her coat where the long plait hung down. And he saw the mismatched eyes that stared at him in anger – one green and one blue.

Without thinking, Rich grabbed the vase from Jade, and hurled it across the room.

The vase struck the woman on the chest. She staggered back, knocking into the heart monitor. The vase shattered on the floor and the flowers were strewn across the bed.

Colonel Shu advanced towards them, holding a scalpel. Jade and Rich backed away. Rich's foot caught on something lying behind him. He looked down quickly to see what it was and saw the plain-clothes police guard – unconscious.

Colonel Shu turned away, just long enough to slice through the tubes and wires keeping Ralph alive. Then she advanced on the twins again.

Rich stepped over the policeman and edged round the far side of the bed. Ralph's breathing was already becoming ragged and laboured. Without taking his eyes off Colonel Shu, Rich lunged for the emergency pull-cord at the head of the bed.

In the distance, a buzzer sounded.

Shu gave a grunt of anger and ran for the door. She swiped the scalpel at Jade as she passed, but Jade easily avoided it – and as she stepped back, Jade kicked out. Her foot connected with Shu's wrist and the scalpel spun away, clattering to the floor.

With another shout of anger, Shu turned and ran.

"Get help," Jade yelled at Rich. "Tell them what happened."

"Where are *you* going?"

"After her."

Rich opened his mouth to protest, but Jade was gone.

Then a hand seized Rich's arm.

2

Jade was in time to see Colonel Shu disappear round the corner at the end of the corridor, her white coat billowing behind her as she ran. Jade set off in pursuit.

Round the corner, the corridor continued past several wards and store rooms. A white coat lay discarded on the floor, but Jade could see the woman's distinctive black pigtail swinging behind her as she ran. There were signs hanging from the ceiling. Colonel Shu was heading for X-Ray, A&E, and the Main Exit.

There was a man mopping the floor. Colonel Shu didn't even slow down; she shoved the man aside and kept running. The mop bucket went flying, spilling grey water across the floor.

"Sorry," said Jade to the man, as she ran past without

helping him up. Her feet were skidding on the slippery wet floor. She slid, and almost fell, but managed to keep going. As soon as she was sure of her balance, she pulled her mobile out of her pocket.

It was switched off. She'd done that when she came into the hospital. It seemed to take forever to turn back on again. As soon as she'd entered her PIN and the handset unlocked, the phone rang.

"Dad?"

"Rich told me," her father's voice said at once. "Where's Shu headed?"

"Trying to get out through Accident and Emergency."

"I'm on it." The phone went dead.

"Yeah," said Jade, stuffing it back in her pocket. "So am I."

There were double doors made of heavy plastic hanging across the end of the corridor. They swung shut behind Shu, their weight almost knocking Jade over as she pushed through.

Shu was already on the other side of the Accident and Emergency waiting area. An elderly woman on crutches was coming through the door. She lurched to one side, somehow remaining upright, as Shu charged past. Then she lost her balance and began to fall. A crutch clattered to the floor.

Jade caught the woman as she fell. She helped her get her balance and picked up her crutch.

"Thank you," the old woman spluttered nervously.

"No problem," Jade told her. "Got to dash."

Through the main doors. Jade skidded to a halt in the glare of the floodlights that illuminated the front of the hospital. A car park stretched away into shadows. Two paramedics were lifting a wheeled stretcher out of the back of an ambulance; its blue lights still flashing. There was no sign of Colonel Shu.

Then the ambulance began to pull away, its back doors flapping. One caught a paramedic on the shoulder as the ambulance moved. He gave a startled yell.

"Who's driving?" the other paramedic shouted in surprise.

Then both were leaping aside, pulling the stretcher out of the way as a car screeched up where the ambulance had just been. It was a silver-grey BMW. The passenger window was open. Through it, Jade could see her dad at the wheel.

Jade wrenched open the door and threw herself into the car.

"Which way?" Chance asked.

Jade pointed. "Follow that ambulance!"

*

Ralph seemed to be unconscious again. He'd given Rich the fright of his life when he sat up and grabbed Rich's arm.

Then the nurses had arrived and sorted out the drips and equipment with an urgent efficiency. Rich left them to it, turning on his mobile phone and calling Chance to warn him about Colonel Shu and tell him Jade was in pursuit.

When he returned to the room, the nurses had finished and a doctor was checking Ralph's vital signs.

"No serious harm done," he assured Rich. "Lucky we weren't a few minutes later, though."

The plain-clothes policeman was slumped in a chair while a nurse dabbed at his bruised head.

Rich cleared up the flowers scattered across the bed, and a nurse gave him a dustpan so he could sweep up the glass. No one said anything, but he got the impression they were more annoyed with him and Jade for making a mess than the woman who had tried to murder their patient.

When he was done, and the policeman had staggered off to make his report, Rich sat down in the visitor's chair beside the bed.

It took him several moments to realise that Ralph's eyes were wide open, and he was looking straight at Rich.

"You're awake," said Rich, startled. "You're OK. I'll get someone."

Ralph's expression didn't change. His eyes were wide and unfocused.

"You *are* OK?" said Rich. He waved his hand in front of Ralph's face. There was no change. Nothing to indicate that Ralph even knew he was there. Until Ralph spoke.

"Flown…" His voice was hoarse and quiet. Rich leaned closer to hear. "Sorry? What do you mean?"

Ralph blinked. His face creased into a frown. Suddenly he was staring right at Rich – really staring at him, focused and alert.

"Tell your father. Tell Ardman." Every word seemed forced out of him.

"Tell them what? That you're awake?"

"If the birds have flown, they will try for the Football." Ralph took a rasping breath of air. "That is what they are planning," he gasped.

Then he slumped back, and his eyes closed.

The heart monitor bleeped forlornly as Ralph slept and Rich wondered what he could have meant.

*

With its back doors still banging and blue lights flashing as it raced through the evening traffic, the ambulance was easy to follow. Until Colonel Shu realised she was being chased and turned off the emergency lights.

Traffic was moving slowly through the busy town centre. As soon as the ambulance lights went off, Chance put his hand on the horn and his foot on the accelerator. He swung the powerful BMW on to the pavement, sending people scattering. Half on the road, half on the pavement, the car roared towards the ambulance making slow progress further ahead.

But before they reached it, the ambulance lights came on again. The siren cut through the evening, and traffic pulled over to let the ambulance through.

The BMW followed in its wake – cutting through the gaps in the traffic before the vehicles had time to move back into the middle of the road.

Jade closed her eyes as they sped through a red light. A car that had braked hard for the ambulance had to do so again. The car behind it slammed into the rear and both cars slewed across the junction. Chance swerved round them, and carried on as if nothing had happened. From behind came the sound of more breaking glass.

Then the sound of more sirens.

"Police," said Chance, glancing in the rear-view mirror. "Just what we don't need."

He slammed the car down a gear to get more power as they raced uphill, along a narrow side street. In front of them the ambulance was spilling equipment and supplies out of its back doors. A car coming the other way caught a glancing blow and spun off on to the pavement, then scraped down the wall of an office block.

The ambulance turned out of the street on to another main road – a dual carriageway. Without hesitation, Chance followed.

"Wrong way!" Jade yelled as the traffic veered off in all directions like the current of a river flowing round a rock.

A huge container lorry was sounding its horn. The ambulance sirens were wailing. The lorry swung across into another lane as it headed towards the ambulance. But the ambulance moved the same way as Colonel Shu tried to avoid the lorry.

The two vehicles collided head-on. The front of the lorry shot up into the air, then crashed down. It landed half across the font of the ambulance. The back of the lorry tilted, the weight of the container dragging it over on to its side.

Chance grabbed the handbrake and the BMW slid

sideways, skidding to a halt right in front of the lorry now sliding sideways towards it.

Jade threw her hands up in front of her face.

Chance rammed the car into gear. The tyres spun, then gripped.

The BMW shot across the road, out of the way of the sliding lorry.

Even before it had stopped, Chance had the door open and was out, running for the half-crushed ambulance. Vehicles skidded to a halt. A police car screeched up beside the ambulance. Uniformed men leaped out and ran to intercept Chance, but he shook them off, and kept running.

By the time Jade got to the ambulance, Chance was waving his identity card at the police and shouting at them to organise a search and close off the area.

The ambulance was empty. Colonel Shu had escaped.

"The local police are not terribly happy," Ardman said.

John Chance and the twins were sitting in Ardman's London office the next morning.

"What are they complaining about?" Rich asked.

Ardman raised an eyebrow. "Well, there's the fact that someone was shot in a restaurant by a renegade Chinese war criminal."

"Oh, right."

"And one of their men was later knocked unconscious by the same renegade war criminal."

"I get the point," said Rich quickly.

But Ardman hadn't finished. He checked a sheet of paper in front of him. "Fourteen cars damaged. A container lorry written off and its cargo destroyed. Television sets apparently. Out of 412 TVs, three survived the crash. Then there's the ambulance. And the hospital equipment Colonel Shu sabotaged. Various driving offences we have told them to drop – including speeding, and going the wrong way down a major dual carriageway. Damage to crash barriers. An old lady who saw the collision had a suspected heart attack, though they do admit that turned out to be indigestion." He paused to peer at the bottom of the sheet. "Oh, and a hospital cleaner sustained a minor bruise on his arm and is threatening to sue."

"Sorry I asked," Rich muttered.

"Having said that," Ardman told them, "I'm more concerned that you let Colonel Shu escape."

"We hardly *let* her escape," Jade told him.

Ardman ignored her. "The second attempt on Ralph's life confirms that his cryptic warning is to be taken seriously. From what his note said, we have to assume there's a nuclear angle."

"He mentioned football as well," said Rich. He'd told the others Ralph's cryptic message – *if the birds have flown, they'll try for the Football.*

Ardman glared. "Yes, and I don't think he was warning us there might be trouble at the European cup final."

"But you do think he's discovered a nuclear threat?" Chance asked quickly before either of his children could respond.

"I do. And there is obviously a connection with the trouble in Wiengwei."

"Do they have nukes?" Rich wondered.

"Not officially. The rebels certainly don't. But as I told you, the Chinese army used to have a nuclear base in the province. It was decommissioned as part of the wider Strategic Arms Limitation agreements over twenty years ago. But there may be a link."

"Worth checking," said Chance. "We need to send someone to Wiengwei to find out whether there's any chance the rebels have acquired a nuclear capability."

Ardman leaned back in his chair and for the first time in the meeting, he smiled. "Just what I thought. In fact, I've decided to send my best man. Right away."

There was silence for a moment.

"But, that's Dad." Jade pointed out.

"We're off to the White House in a couple of days," Rich added.

"To see the President," Jade continued. "You promised. And Dad promised."

Ardman held up his hands for silence. "We have an excellent contact in Wiengwei. A friend of Ralph's in fact, so he's keen to help. And apparently Ralph was there recently organising some deal or other, so that's another connection. One that might explain how he found out whatever it is that he found out. All you need to do," he told Chance, "is check in with this man on the way. The flights are arranged."

"Flights?" said Chance.

"It's on the way to Washington. Sort of. Well, given your schedule, it'll have to be. It also gets all three of you well away from Colonel Shu. She may know who you are now, and Goddard's team can track her down while you're well out of the way."

"Wait a minute," said Rich. "What do you mean, *all three*? You don't expect me and Jade to go to Wiengwei as well, do you?"

"I'm afraid so," said Ardman. "I really can't afford to

organise two flights to the same place. Not with over 400 televisions to pay for suddenly. You'll leave the spying to your dad, of course." He raised his eyebrows, as if he didn't rate the chances of that.

"But we still get to go to the White House reception, right?" Jade wanted to be sure. "All of us?"

"Of course. You can stop off in Wiengwei to refuel, have a quick chat with our friend Mr Chang, and be in Washington in good time for the White House reception. You should have a day or two to spare to see the sights. If it all goes smoothly."

"Any reason why it shouldn't?" Chance asked.

Ardman smiled. "None at all."

"Terrific," Jade muttered.

3

They changed planes in Hong Kong, where they also picked up tourist visas that Ardman had arranged for China. Given his worry about cost, Jade suspected they might not have been issued through the 'usual channels'. From Hong Kong they got a direct flight to Weijiang, the main city of Wiengwei province.

Immigration seemed to take an age, but otherwise there were no problems. They only had hand luggage as Ardman had sent their cases direct to Washington on an RAF flight. Jade wondered if that meant there was actually more or less chance of their luggage arriving when and where it was supposed to.

Chance, Rich and Jade eventually emerged into a large open area where there were a few small shops selling food and newspapers. Through the main doors they could see several cars parked at the kerb.

An old woman carrying a basket pushed past Jade. She was surprised and saddened to see that there was a live chicken cramped inside the basket, grey feathers poking out through the weave.

"Lots of signs," said Rich. "But they're not much help. They're all in Chinese."

"Maybe Dad can read them?" said Jade.

"This way," Chance decided, and set off across the airport.

"You *can* read Chinese!" said Jade, impressed.

"No. But I can read English."

The sign actually said 'ENGLISH'. It was written in block capitals on a sheet of grey cardboard using a chunky marker pen. It was being held by a small boy of about twelve years old. He had short, dark hair, and enormous front teeth that he was showing off in a broad smile.

As Chance, Jade and Rich approached, the smile got even broader and the boy bobbed up and down with excitement.

"Yoshi!" he exclaimed as they reached him. "Yoshi!" He bowed abruptly and quickly.

Jade bowed back. "Yoshi!" she replied, echoing his greeting.

Rich copied her. "Yoshi!"

The boy's smile faded. Then it reappeared and he bowed again. "Yoshi!" He straightened up and tapped his chest with his finger. "Yoshi!"

"Your turn, Dad," said Rich.

"Yeah, don't be rude," Jade told him.

Dad dutifully bowed his head. "John Chance," he said. Then he smiled at Rich and Jade. "Yoshi is his *name*."

The boy grabbed Jade's holdall from her before she could object. In exchange he gave her the cardboard sign. Then he hurried off across the airport.

"Are we being mugged?" Rich wondered, grinning.

"He wants us to follow him," said Jade.

"Really? You think?"

"Children!" said Chance, sternly. But he was smiling too as they all followed Yoshi to the main exit.

Outside, the temperature was about the same as it had been in London when they left – mild, but not warm. There was a light drizzle that hung like mist in the air. Yoshi was opening the boot of a battered car waiting at the kerb, its engine humming. He dumped Jade's bag inside and gestured for Rich and Chance to put their bags in the boot too. Then he slammed the boot closed and hurried round to the front of the car.

"He's never driving," said Jade as Yoshi opened the right-hand front door of the car and got in.

As she spoke, a man in the other front seat turned to look at them. He was laughing.

"Left-hand drive in Wiengwei," he said.

Mr Chang was like a larger version of his son Yoshi. His smile was semi-permanent, and his hair was thinning and edged with white. He explained he had not come into the airport to meet them himself because if he stopped the car it took for ever to get it started again. As he drove, threading his way between a mass of bicycles, he spoke over his shoulder to Chance, Jade and Rich who were jammed in the back.

"I have been making inquiries. Discreet inquiries of course. The man who will know the answers to your questions runs a factory in the city. We go there now, and he is expecting us. OK?"

"OK," Chance agreed. "What have you told him?"

"About you? Nothing. I have allowed him to assume you are French. I will translate, and he won't know English from French from Greek."

"How does he get his information?" Jade asked.

"He has contacts in the Chinese military. He gets things for the soldiers. Cigarettes, drink, magazines."

"Smut," Jade muttered.

"*Newsweek*, Hong Kong edition," Mr Chang corrected her. "Books too. My friend will know whether nuclear missiles were really ever stationed in Wiengwei, and if so where. The declaration the Chinese government made at the disarmament talks was rather vague and may have been a bluff anyway. But there are certainly many military bases in the province."

"Despite the rebels?" Rich asked.

"Because of the rebels. Some of the bases have been taken over by the rebels."

In the front passenger seat, Yoshi suddenly spoke up excitedly.

"What did he say?" Jade asked when the boy had finished.

Mr Chang laughed. "He says he has never met westerners before. He says he thinks you are very nice. And he is fascinated by the yellow colour of your hair. He asks if it is dyed."

"Tell him no," said Jade.

"And tell him we think he's very nice too," Rich added. "Especially my sister."

*

Mr Chang didn't really park the car. He just stopped it in the road and got out.

"We try not to attract too much attention," he said. "Yoshi has baseball caps for you. Wear them low, so people cannot easily see your hair and eyes. Your height might be more difficult to disguise."

"Expecting trouble?" Chance asked.

"Only getting my car to start again. But you are distinctive. The less attention you attract, the better. We don't get westerners here as a rule."

"Except US airmen falling from the sky," said Rich. No one knew what had happened to the crew of the crashed plane, but he didn't fancy ending up in the next cell.

Mr Chang nodded. "Rumour has it, the plane was shot down."

"It was over Chinese airspace," Chance admitted.

"With permission, the Americans say," Jade pointed out.

"Parts of this province are a war zone," said Mr Chang. "Who knows what really happened, or where the airmen are now?"

Even with the baseball caps, it seemed as though everyone was looking at them as they followed Mr Chang and Yoshi. Rich was aware of people turning, staring and talking to each other as he passed. Bicycles wobbled as they went by. People called out, but Mr Chang ignored them.

Further up the road, Mr Chang led them down a side street, which seemed to have been turned into an impromptu market. There was hardly room to get through between the stalls. People were selling hot food from the back of carts, cotton and other fabrics from trestle tables, watches and pens, even a few iPods.

The smell was awful. Rich could only guess what Jade was thinking as they passed cages of chickens and song birds, a pen with piglets grunting round inside, and several mangy-looking goats.

Mr Chang and Yoshi waved away all offers of goods and bargains and forged a path through the market. Finally they emerged at the other end of the narrow street. Mr Chang pushed open a plain, metal door set into the brick wall of a nondescript building and they went inside.

The noise was incredible. For as far as Rich could see, the building was one enormous room, filled with people working on sewing machines. There were a few men, but mainly women and children. Mr Chang led the way along the side of the room.

"What are they all doing?" Rich asked.

"They make clothes for export to the West," Mr Chang explained.

"A sweatshop," said Jade angrily.

"Careful, Jade," her father warned.

"Well it is," she retorted. "I bet they get paid almost nothing."

"Not much," Mr Chang agreed. "But at least they have work."

"Hey," said Rich, as they passed a woman sewing a collar on to a brightly coloured blouse. "You've got one like that, Jade."

"It's going to a charity shop as soon as I get back," she told him.

There was a door at the end of the factory floor that led into an office area. Mr Chang and Chance went through to another office, leaving Yoshi with Rich and Jade.

"I hope Dad's going to tell the boss just what he thinks of this place," said Jade.

"I hope he's not," Rich told her. "At least, not until he's found out about the nukes."

Yoshi grinned at them and said something they didn't understand. But Jade smiled back at him encouragingly.

"At least you don't have to work in a place like this," she said.

"Yeah," Rich agreed, "at least your dad's a decadent western spy whose mates sell booze and ciggies to the troops. You stick with it, kid." He winked at Jade. "In a place like this," he said, more serious now, "I think they just have to survive however they can. Especially with a rebellion going on."

"I guess so. Doesn't mean it's a good thing though."

"No, it doesn't," said Rich.

Chance waited until they were back in the car before he told them how the meeting with Mr Chang's contact had gone.

"There was a Chinese People's Liberation Army nuclear base about 150 kilometres outside the city. The nukes were all decommissioned and there's just a small force left to guard the place."

"So we can get going, then," said Rich. "Washington, here we come!"

"If we're going anywhere," said Jade, as Mr Chang kept trying to start the car. The engine coughed and spluttered, then died.

"Soon. Mr Chang's contact says there's been unusual

activity at the base recently. Convoys of lorries and increased security. It is also in the area where Mr Chang says Ralph had some business contacts."

"So you want to go and take a look?" Jade guessed.

"Seems sensible."

"Seems suicidal," she said. "You can't just wander in and ask if they've got any old nukes left or whether the rebels have taken them all."

Chance held up two small plastic cards. "Actually, I can. These are high-level security passes for a military inspection team. Mr Chang and I are going in to take a look round. If we ever get going."

The engine finally caught and Mr Chang smiled and gave them a thumbs up.

"Just the two passes?" Rich asked as they pulled away.

"That was all he could get," said Chance, rather too quickly.

"You mean it's all you asked for," said Jade.

Mr Chang cleared his throat. "Paid for, actually. They were not cheap."

"Nothing is," said Jade. "Except slave labour."

"And what do we do while you're gate-crashing the Chinese People's Liberation Army Former Nuclear Base Party?" Rich wanted to know.

"I have a sister who lives not far from the base," said Mr Chang. "She will look after you. She is a good cook. And Yoshi is good at eating." He said something to Yoshi, who grinned, and mimed shovelling food into his mouth.

They left the car at Mr Chang's sister's house. It was little more than a wooden hut, with a living space that obviously doubled as a bedroom, and a little kitchen off that. There was a toilet and washroom, which were surprisingly sophisticated compared with the antiquated kitchen. Chang's sister bowed in welcome and loosed off a barrage of fast, unintelligible conversation.

Chance and Mr Chang changed into Chinese military uniforms that Mr Chang's contact at the clothes factory had also provided. Chance had to struggle into his uniform, and the jacket wouldn't do up. But he made a passable Chinese soldier. They set off on foot as the evening was drawing in, and were soon lost to sight.

"Right," said Jade as soon as they were gone, "the big question is, can we persuade Yoshi to show us the way to this base?"

Rich shook his head. "No way. The big question is, how quickly can Yoshi's aunt cook us some food before he shows us the way to this base?"

"Actually, the big question is whether we can make Yoshi understand what we're asking," Jade decided.

The boy was standing beside them outside the little house. For once, he wasn't smiling. He pointed at Jade, then he pointed at Rich, and then he pointed at himself.

"Us, all of us, yes?" said Jade.

Yoshi pointed to them all again, then he pointed down the road in the direction his father and Chance had gone. He mimed walking on the spot.

"All of us, follow them," Rich interpreted. "Looks like language isn't a barrier after all." He bent down to talk to the boy. "We need to tell your aunt that we're going out. And any chance of something to eat first? I'm starving."

Yoshi shrugged and shook his head. He obviously had no idea what Rich was asking.

They got through the main gates with no problem. If the guard wondered how the two official inspectors from Army HQ had got to the base on foot, he knew better than to ask.

Mr Chang did the talking, while Chance kept his head down – literally, so his face could not be seen under his uniform cap. He also tried to hunch up and appear shorter than he really was. The guard opened the barrier and let them walk into the base.

As well as several outbuildings and workshops, there was an administration block and a large hangar. Chance set off for the hangar. In the dying light of the evening he could see grass growing through the concrete slabs that made up the roadway. The whole place looked run down and dilapidated. Some of the admin block windows were boarded up, and the doors to the hangar looked like they were rusted open.

"I don't think our passes will allow us into the main silos and more secure areas," said Mr Chang.

"There's hardly anyone here," Chance pointed out. "The place has been all but abandoned. With luck we can be in and out again before anyone even notices. Or if they do, no one will miss them for a few hours."

"Sounds easy enough," Mr Chang agreed. "And the guard at the gate is obviously not expecting any trouble. He says most of the troops were moved out a few weeks ago, and he thinks the rest of them have been forgotten and left to rot."

"He may well be right. I doubt anyone else ever comes here."

They reached the hangar and went inside. There was a

guard standing beside a large, metal door with a locking wheel.

"Looks like that's where we want to go," said Chance.

The guard was walking towards them, gesturing angrily and shouting. Mr Chang shouted back, but the guard didn't seem impressed. He advanced on them, rifle at the ready.

"He says this is a restricted area and only the base commander and duty guard are allowed in here," said Mr Chang, quietly.

"Don't worry," Chance told him. "Let me explain."

As soon as the guard was within reach, Chance grabbed the end of the man's rifle, ripped it from his grip, swung it round and slammed it into the guard's head. The man dropped silently to the floor.

"I think he got the message," said Chance. He checked the soldier's pulse, and then slung the assault rifle over his shoulder. "Sorry about that," he murmured.

It took both of them to heave open the heavy metal door. On the other side, a metal stairway led down into blackness. Mr Chang handed Chance a torch, and produced another one for himself from his jacket pocket.

"Thank you, Mr Chang. You think of everything. Now, let's see what's downstairs."

Up above ground, more unexpected visitors were arriving at the base.

The first visitors were three children. They crouched in the darkness just off the main road, watching the guard at the gate.

"We'll never get past him," said Jade.

"The place looks pretty run-down, but the security fence looks intact," said Rich.

"Think Dad's in there?"

Rich nodded. "Oh yeah."

"Think he needs help?"

"Doubt it."

From behind them came the sound of approaching vehicles. Rich, Jade and Yoshi drew back from the roadside as lights cut through the darkness. Two massive army trucks were rumbling towards the base.

The guard was standing in the middle of the road, in front of the wooden barrier. In the glare of the headlights, Rich could see that he looked confused, worried and surprised.

Then he dived to one side as the front truck picked up speed – heading straight for the gate. The truck crashed through, the second truck close behind it. The first truck kept going, towards the distant hangar and admin block. The second turned in a wide arc and stopped.

Uniformed figures leaped from the back of the second truck. The guard from the gate was running towards them, shouting, his rifle levelled.

He was still shouting when the newcomers opened fire. The guard was thrown back by the impacting bullets.

The other side of the gate, in the near-darkness, Yoshi tugged at Rich's sleeve. His face was pale with fear. He said something, a single word. Rich could guess what it meant.

"Rebels," said Jade.

Rich nodded. "*Now* Dad needs help."

4

Huge arc lights flickered on. They illuminated the whole area in a harsh, white glow. Dark figures emerged from the admin block and barracks at the far side of the base. The two trucks had stopped not far from them, and the newcomers returned fire.

"Let's hope he's not caught in the middle of that," said Rich.

"He'll be in the hangar," Jade replied. She had to shout over the sound of gunfire. "He's looking for missiles, remember."

Yoshi was talking rapidly and urgently. But Rich had no idea what he was saying.

"You'd better get home," he told the boy. He pointed back up the road, the way they had come. "Go! Stay safe.

Me and Jade will try to help, OK?" He pointed to himself and Jade, then into the base as he spoke.

Yoshi said something else, nodding the whole time. He grabbed Rich's hand and shook it. He stood on tiptoe and kissed Jade on the cheek. Then he turned and ran, disappearing into the darkness.

"Think he understood?" Jade asked.

"I think he likes you."

Jade ignored him. "Let's get to that hangar and find Dad."

Fortunately the fighting was well away from the hangar. The rebels were sheltering behind their trucks, firing on the troops from the base. But taken by surprise, the base soldiers were at a disadvantage.

A streak of fire shot out from beside one of the trucks, then slammed into the brick-built admin block. The whole building seemed to light up as the rocket exploded. Windows were blown out and bodies went flying.

"Won't be long before they head for the hangar," Rich gasped as he and Jade ran. "Come on!"

They paused for a moment inside the hangar, and let their eyes adjust from the brighter light outside to the interior gloom. As soon as he got his breath back, Rich tried to push the heavy doors closed, but they wouldn't move.

Jade was crouching over a prone figure. "Looks like someone got here before us."

Rich hurried to join her. "I can guess who. Dad."

"Yeah, the guard's just out cold. The rebels would have shot him."

"So where have Dad and Mr Chang gone?"

The hangar was enormous, but it was almost empty. There was a jeep and a couple of other vehicles, but nowhere much for anyone to hide. In any case, they'd have seen Rich and Jade arrive.

"The way he's facing…" said Jade. "When he fell, he was heading towards the main doors."

"Like he was coming to meet someone," Rich agreed. "So trace his path back…"

They both saw the large metal door set into the hangar wall, and ran over to it. The door was standing slightly open, and together they heaved on it. Once through they closed it again. They were standing in a dark stairwell. The only light was a faint glow from far below.

"Guess where we're going," said Rich.

The night was getting cold and Yoshi didn't like the dark. He was alone and afraid, but he knew what he had to do. He kept to the darkest shadows, out of the pale moonlight that filtered through the clouds.

He ran all the way, hoping he would recognise the point where he needed to turn off the main road and take the narrow track that led back to his aunt's house. He was gasping for breath, but he kept going – he couldn't let his father down. He couldn't abandon his father's friends, the boy and the girl and their father…

It seemed to take an age, but at last he could see the dark shape of his aunt's house ahead. Yoshi paused for a moment. He had to stop, to get his breath back. He stood gasping, hands on his knees, shivering from the cold and the fear. Gradually he caught his breath; slowly he straightened up. Only then did he see a man standing a few metres away.

A man with a gun.

The sound of gunfire from outside was muffled. It grew quieter as they descended deep into the ground. The glow from below was getting brighter and Rich could tell it was electric light.

The metal steps were rusted and insecure. The whole stairway wobbled alarmingly, and they kept close to the wall as they picked their way down.

After an age, they finally reached the bottom. A

corridor stretched away ahead of them, bare bulbs hanging from the ceiling. About half of them were lit, and Rich guessed the bulbs had gone in the others. Cables and pipes ran along the walls and the roof. Water dripped into oily puddles on the concrete floor, and the whole place felt clammy and cold.

There was a body at the bottom of the stairs – another unconscious soldier. Again, there was no sign of his weapon, if he'd had one.

"Still on the right track, then," Jade whispered.

All they could hear was the dripping of water and a faint hum that might be a distant generator. No sound could be heard from above.

"We'd better hurry," said Rich. "Dad won't know there's a battle going on above ground."

"I don't fancy being trapped down here if the rebels come after us," said Jade.

Together they hurried along the damp passageway. It turned a corner, and continued into the distance. At the far end, Rich could just make out the dark shape of a doorway.

A figure leaped out from the shadows close in front of them. The light was behind him, but Rich could make out the Chinese army uniform. A rifle swung up to cover

Rich and Jade as they skidded to a halt.

Another shape detached itself from the shadows beside them. Another uniformed figure holding a rifle.

"Come to join us?" Mr Chang queried, lowering his rifle.

"What the hell are you doing here?" Chance asked.

Rich gasped with relief. "Rebels – attacking the base."

"We thought we should warn you," said Jade. "There's a battle going on up there. They've got guns, rocket launchers, the lot."

"And I'm guessing they'll be coming down here as soon as they've sorted out the troops on the base," added Rich.

"You're probably right," Chance conceded.

"Where's Yoshi?" Mr Chang asked.

"We sent him home," said Jade. "We couldn't bring him in here, and put him in danger."

Mr Chang shrugged. "He has black belt in karate."

"Wouldn't help him stop a bullet," said Rich.

"True," Mr Chang agreed. "Thank you."

"So what are the rebels after?" Jade asked. "If this base is decommissioned and pretty much abandoned, what's here they could want?"

Chance gestured for them to follow and led the way along the corridor to the open door at the end. Beyond was blackness. As he stepped through the door, Rich could feel a chill, like he was standing inside a vast, empty chamber.

Beside him, Mr Chang was fumbling on the wall beside the door. There was a *clunk* as he found the connection for the lights and pushed the lever that closed the circuit. High above, enormous lamps flickered into life.

Rich had been right. The place was huge – a massive chamber hewn out of the rock. The bare walls were dripping with moisture. The floor was an expanse of cracked and pitted concrete, with gantries and walkways stretching across the roof space high above.

But the chamber wasn't empty. An enormous missile stood like a pillar, reaching almost to the large circular hatch in the roof above. It was rusting, with faded Chinese stars emblazoned on its side.

"A Dong-Feng series 4 launcher," said Mr Chang, quietly.

"NATO calls it the CSS-3," Chance added. "Built in the 1980s, and then superseded. It's probably been abandoned."

"Nuclear?" Jade asked in a whisper.

"Oh yes," Chance told them. "With a range of near

enough 5,000 kilometres, accurate to within 500 metres. And a warhead that delivers between thirty and forty megatons."

"I guess that's what the rebels are after," said Rich.

"This and another dozen we've found in other silos. Whatever happens, they mustn't get them. Not even one of them."

From the other end of the long corridor came the unmistakable sound of a heavy metal door crashing open.

5

"We're going to need some help," said Rich.

"I called in backup as soon as we found the missiles," Chance told them. "Weak signal, but there's an extraction team ready in India. It'll take them hours to get here, though. With the rebels on their way, we're on our own."

"You know how to disable a nuclear missile?" Jade asked.

"It's never too late to learn."

"You are kidding."

Chance shrugged. "Afraid not."

In the distance they could hear the thump of booted feet on the metal stairway.

"I think we should hurry," Mr Chang told them. "The rebels are coming, remember?"

"Right," Chance decided. "Let's take a closer look at the problem."

He set off for a metal ladder leading up to the walkways above. It seemed in better condition than the stairs they had come down, and soon all four of them were climbing.

"They don't know we're here," said Jade. "They're looking for the missiles. We could hide."

"What about the unconscious soldiers?" said Rich. "They'll know someone's down here."

At the top of the ladder, a metal gantry led across towards the top of the missile. There were railings along each side, but they were rusty and corroded.

Rich looked down, feeling his stomach lurch when he saw how high they were.

"If they try and launch that thing, it'll probably explode," he said. "It's so old and neglected."

"They will remove the warhead and use another delivery method," said Mr Chang.

"Can *we* remove it?" Jade wondered. "Get the warheads away from here?"

"No, we can't," Chance called back over his shoulder. He was almost at the nose of the rocket. One of the large strip lights was shining in their eyes, so the rocket was just a hazy blur.

"Why not?"

"First, because it's far too heavy. And second…"

The roof was just a metre above their heads. The walkway turned to circle the rocket. There were massive hinges holding it to the wall, and Rich guessed it would be swung away when the missile launched. It was obviously positioned there for maintenance, allowing engineers to get close enough to work on the nose cone.

Except there was no nose cone. The top of the rocket was an empty cylinder, with wires and cables spilling out.

"And second," Chance finished, "because someone's already taken the warhead away."

"So, the missiles *were* decommissioned," said Mr Chang. "The rebels will be rather disappointed, if they're all like this."

"I'll bet they are," said Jade. "But we don't have time to check."

Far below, uniformed men were running into the silo. They spread out through the open space, checking everywhere, guns at the ready.

"We're too close to the light for them to see us," said Chance. "That's why we couldn't see the warhead was gone. And neither can they."

"But they'll soon come and look," Rich told him. "And there's no way we can get down without them spotting us."

Jade was leaning over the top of the missile, braced against the rusting handrails. "Look at this."

"What is it?" Chance hurried to join her.

"Oil. Recently spilled. And the edges of the wires where they've been cut – they're still shiny, like new."

"You mean, this was recent?" Rich asked.

"Can't be more than a day or two since the warhead was removed," Chance agreed. "The rebels must have known they were still here, and they're only just too late. That's what Ralph was warning us about, I bet – that the rebels were planning to get the missiles. Seems the Chinese knew that too and finally acted – got the warheads to safety before the rebels could take them."

"So where are the warheads now?" Jade wondered.

"There was a convoy," said Mr Chang. "Yesterday, my contact at the factory told me, a lot of soldiers and vehicles left this base."

"You didn't mention that," said Chance.

Mr Chang shrugged. "I told you they had left only a small force behind. It didn't seem important. But now…"

"The nukes can't be far away. They might still be in

Wiengwei. They're too big to fly out on a cargo plane, so they must have left by road, on big, slow, cumbersome trucks. And the rebels will soon be after them."

"Once they've finished with us," Rich whispered. "Look!"

He pointed to where the first rebel troops were climbing up the metal ladders towards the walkway.

There was another ladder leading down from the other end of the walkway, but rebel soldiers were climbing that one as well.

"There's no other way down," said Jade.

Rich stared at the rocket. Something had occurred to him, though it wasn't a thought he relished. "What about *up*?"

"Up?!" Jade stared at him.

"The roof must open when they launch the missiles. There must be a way out."

"That hatch," said Chance.

There was a huge circular hatch that they had seen from the ground. But it was tight shut.

"How do we get it open?" Mr Chang asked.

"Ideas soon, please," Jade hissed.

The first rebels were almost at the top of the ladders.

"Manual controls?" Chance wondered. "Look –

everyone look, see if there's a switch or a lever or a button. Anything."

"I bet the controls are down there," said Rich, pointing over the side of the walkway. "I mean, you wouldn't want to be operating controls up here when it launched would you?"

"Doesn't matter now anyway," said Jade.

The first of the rebel troops had spotted them. He was shielding his eyes from the bright glare of the lights with one hand, and holding his rifle level in the other. He shouted at them.

"He's asking who we are. He can't see us clearly," said Mr Chang quietly. "What do we do?"

"We ask them to open the hatch for us to escape," said Chance.

"Oh, like that'll help," said Jade.

"Tell him we're on his side," Chance told Mr Chang. "Then shout to them down below to open the hatch so they can get the warhead off the missile."

"Are you serious?" Rich asked.

"Worth a try," Chance told him as Mr Chang shouted to the approaching rebel soldiers. They shouted back angrily. The leading rebel raised his rifle.

Mr Chang yelled urgently at him. Then he leaned over

71

the walkway and shouted down – urgent and loud. There was an answering shout, and Mr Chang yelled the same thing again, even more loudly.

He turned to the others. "I think it's working. They said that—"

But his words were drowned out by the sound of the enormous hatchway above the missile sliding back. Through it, the black night sky was visible. A cool breeze riffled Rich's hair.

"I can't believe they fell for that," said Rich.

"Move," said Chance. "They won't fall for it for long." He grabbed Jade and hoisted her up bodily into the gap a metre above his head. She grabbed the edge and hauled herself out, reaching back for Rich.

Just then, there was another shout from below. Moments later, a bullet pinged off the walkway.

"I think," said Mr Chang drily, "they have detected our ruse."

Rich watched from on top of the roof as Chance raised his rifle and took careful aim – not at the rebel soldiers but at the wall of the silo, where the walkway was fixed.

The sound of the shot was deafening.

The rebel soldiers charged along the walkway, not daring to fire in case they hit the warhead.

Chance fired again, this time a burst of automatic fire. The huge hinges broke away from their fixings, and the walkway lurched to one side. Mr Chang jumped back from the edge as the walkway tipped.

Further along, the effect was more pronounced. The metal was twisting, ripping apart under its own weight now it was no longer attached to the silo wall. The rebel soldier fired. But as he loosed off the shot, his feet skidded from under him and he pitched over the side of the walkway with a cry.

Gunfire pinged off the rim of the hatch. There was more shouting. Rich reached down and grabbed hold of Mr Chang's arms, helping to pull him up through the open hatch.

Then there was a grinding sound as the hatch began to close again. Rich hurried to help Jade, who was reaching back down into the silo for their father. He was firing at the oncoming rebels, now approaching from the other direction where the walkway still held. They ducked away as bullets ricocheted off the side of the missile.

Chance let off a final burst, then flung the rifle up and out of the closing hole in the roof. He leaped after it. His hands grabbed the edge of the hatchway. Jade and Rich struggled to secure his arms and pull him up and through.

The hatch was closing fast. Tonnes of metal sliced towards Chance as he desperately tried to haul himself out of the way. Finally – just as it seemed he was too late – he managed to heave himself up and out. His foot came clear of the hatch just as it closed.

"Thanks," he gasped. "I thought for a moment I was going to be de-feeted!"

Getting away from the silo was relatively easy. The rebels were busy dealing with the last of the Chinese army troops, or down in the silos looking for nuclear warheads that were no longer there.

"We'll head back to Mr Chang's sister's," Chance decided. "The extraction team can pick us up there, and we can make sure Yoshi is all right."

"He'll be fine," Mr Chang assured them. But his smile looked forced and Jade knew he must be worried about the boy.

The trouble started just as they were leaving the base. One of the rebel trucks was starting up. Its headlights picked out Jade and the others as it swung round on to the main roadway and headed for the gates.

There was a shout, followed by gunfire.

"They're telling us to stop," said Mr Chang.

"Warning shots. They're aiming to miss," said Chance, "which is good."

"They think we know where the warheads have gone," Mr Chang told him, after listening to shouts from the rebels. "Which is bad."

There were more shots, which again went wide. Chance pulled a mobile phone from his pocket. Jade could see the display showed a crude map, with two flashing symbols. She guessed one must be the phone itself. The other was a small graphic of a helicopter.

"Twenty-two minutes," Chance announced. "Keep running!"

He turned as he ran, loosing off a burst of gunfire. One of the truck's headlamps exploded into fragments and went out. Answering gunfire chewed up the concrete close to his feet.

"This way!" said Mr Chang as he headed off the road, into the thick undergrowth to one side and into dense woodland.

Jade followed, aware of her father and Rich close behind her. They kept running. There was the sound of people following. Some of the rebels had obviously been dropped off from the truck and were coming after them.

"How long now?" Rich gasped after what seemed an age.

"Fifteen minutes."

"We are nearly back at my sister's," Mr Chang announced.

"That might not help," said Chance.

Jade could see torches shining in the dense woodland behind them and heard shouting. It wouldn't be long before the rebels caught up with them.

At last they broke out of the woodland and found themselves back on the road where it cut through the trees. On the other side, the wood continued, as dense and forbidding as ever.

"Ten minutes," Chance announced.

"This way!" Mr Chang started along the road. Then he stopped abruptly.

Dark figures were rising up all around. There was the unmistakable sound of rifles being readied. One of the figures shouted urgently at Mr Chang. Rebel soldiers burst out of the woodland behind Jade, their torches picking her out and illuminating Rich and Chance.

The single remaining headlight of the rebel truck cut through the night as it turned on to the narrow road a hundred metres away and rumbled towards Jade, Rich, Chance and Mr Chang.

6

The dark figures closest to Jade – the ones who had shouted to Mr Chang – opened fire. But they weren't shooting at Jade, Rich, Chance and Mr Chang. They were firing into the woodland, driving back the pursuing rebels.

The truck was still approaching. Its remaining headlight exploded and the windscreen shattered. It slewed off the road.

"This way!" Mr Chang shouted, leading them across the road and into the trees on the other side.

"Keep running," Chance yelled. "There's a clearing in a few hundred metres."

"Who are these people?" Jade gasped, looking at the dark figures running with them.

They were dressed in black – not uniforms, but jeans and jerseys. Their faces were smeared with dark camouflage paint.

"My brother-in-law and his friends," Mr Chang called back to her as they ran.

"But how did they know…"

Jade broke off as she felt a small hand grab her own. She looked down to see Yoshi grinning up at her. His face was also smeared black and he was wearing a dark jersey several sizes too large for him.

"Oh," said Jade. "Right. Hi, Yoshi. And thanks!"

"Nice one!" Rich exclaimed, and slapped the small boy on the back – almost knocking him over. But Yoshi just laughed.

They kept running. They could see torch lights behind them and flashes from gun muzzles. Bullets hammered into the ground and the trunks of the trees. One of the black-clad figures gave a yell and pitched forwards. Immediately he was grabbed by two of his friends. One hoisted him on to his shoulder and they kept going, returning fire as they went.

From above came the sound of an engine. A searchlight cut through the night, lighting up the woodland. It seemed to hover a short distance ahead of them.

"Helicopter!" Chance shouted.

They burst out of the woods into a wide clearing. The helicopter was just landing in front of them.

"It's not big enough for all of us," Jade yelled above the sound of the rotors.

"We will hold off the rebels until you are gone," Mr Chang shouted back. "Don't worry about us. We know these woods and can vanish into them like that." The snap of his fingers was lost in the noise.

The black-clad fighters had taken up position round the clearing and were firing back into the woodland.

"Time for you to go!" Mr Chang shouted. He shook hands with Chance, then with Rich and Jade.

"Will Yoshi be OK?" Jade asked.

As she spoke, a rebel in camouflage uniform broke from the woods off to one side. Somehow he had got through Mr Chang's cordon. He brought up his gun, aiming at the helicopter.

But before he could fire, a small, dark figure slammed into him. There was a whirl of arms and the gun went flying. The rebel landed on his back, and lay still.

"I think he'll be fine, Jade," said Rich as Yoshi ran back towards them.

Yoshi stopped in front of them, and bowed. Rich and

Jade quickly bowed back. Chance reached out and shook Yoshi's hand. Then he turned to Mr Chang and said something to him. But Jade didn't hear above the gunfire and the helicopter.

A man had jumped down from the helicopter and was waving for them to hurry up. It was Dex Halford – a colleague of their father's that Jade and Rich knew well. They'd been in some pretty tight situations together. Despite being invalided out of the SAS when he lost a leg below the knee, Halford was still a tough professional.

"Come on!" Chance shouted. "Let's not keep the taxi waiting."

They ran for the helicopter, ducking low to avoid the whirling rotor blades. Halford helped them inside.

"Good to see you."

Chance leaned over to say something to Halford, speaking close to his ear. Halford shook his head.

"What is it?" Rich asked.

The helicopter was beginning to lift. Jade waved to Mr Chang and Yoshi through the open door.

"Why are they waiting there?" she wondered. "Why don't they get under cover like everyone else?"

Halford was still talking urgently to Chance, hand on his shoulder. Now it was Chance's turn to shake his head.

Then he turned to Rich and Jade. "Enjoy the White House!" he yelled above the growing noise of the engines. "If I'm not back in time, Dex can take you!"

"What?!" Jade shouted back.

"Unfinished business."

"What do you mean?" Rich demanded. "You're coming with us."

The helicopter was three metres off the ground and rising.

John Chance smiled at his children. He nodded at Dex Halford, and leaped from the open door down to the ground receding below. He rolled like a paratrooper and was back on his feet. He turned to wave just once, then he was running for cover with Yoshi and Mr Chang as the rebel soldiers burst out of the woodland, guns blazing.

The helicopter search light went off, and it turned in the darkness. Keeping low to avoid being detected by radar, it headed for the nearest border.

"Sometimes," Jade told Rich, "I could kill him."

He nodded. "Let's hope no one beats us to it."

The Davison Hotel in Washington DC was a stark contrast to the accommodation in Wiengwei. Rich and Jade each had their own suite of rooms, with a connecting door between them. Halford had another suite across the corridor.

Although he'd managed to get some sleep on the flight, Rich was tired. He had a shower, then collapsed into bed. When he was woken by the sound of his bedside phone, he was surprised to see he'd been asleep for several hours. They had arrived in the early morning, and it was now past lunch time.

He grabbed the phone, expecting it to be the hotel manager welcoming him and telling him how good the place was. Instead Rich heard a voice he recognised.

"Hi there, sleepyhead. Your sister and Mr Halford are wondering if you're up to a quick tour of the sights."

Chuck White was waiting with Halford and Jade in the hotel lobby. He was a big, broad-shouldered man and Rich knew he was in the Secret Service team that protected the US President. Rich didn't think he'd ever seen Chuck White out of a suit or uniform. Now he was wearing jeans and a casual jacket.

"Got today off," he told Rich, shaking his hand warmly. "Thought I'd offer to be your tour guide, if you're up to it. Been to Washington before?"

Despite living in the USA for years with their mum, Rich and Jade had only been to Washington DC once before, and that was years ago. They gratefully accepted the offer of a tour.

"Is Kate Hunter joining us?" Jade wondered.

They'd got to know both Chuck and Kate just recently, and even been stranded in the deserts of Iraq together.

Rich was disappointed when Chuck shook his head. "She's out of town, I'm afraid. Taking care of a little business in New York State." Chuck clapped his hands together. "So, where do you guys want to start? Lincoln Memorial? Smithsonian? We even have an International Spy Museum down near Chinatown."

"No, thanks," Halford told him. "We're on holiday. No spying allowed."

In the conference room of a rather less expensive hotel in upstate New York, a meeting was taking place.

A dozen men and several women sat round a large conference table that was peppered with cigarette burns and stained with coffee rings. They waited with a mixture of nervousness and excitement for the man who had just come into the room to speak.

He was average height, with very ordinary short brown hair. His face was the sort that people immediately forgot as soon as they looked away. He had no distinctive features at all, except for his voice.

When he spoke it was a sound somewhere between a croak and a whisper. Everyone in the room leaned forward slightly, eager to catch every word he said. His voice was quiet, commanding and frightening.

"I lied," the man said, standing at the head of the conference table. He waited for his words to sink in. "Now that Tom has collected all your cell phones, and we're about to get on the bus, I can tell you what's really going on."

The man leaned forward, knuckles pressing down on the table. "We all know that the new cold war has already started. And if we don't heat it up, the Chinese sure as hell will. They've already started by holding our airmen without trial. Hell, they won't even admit they've got them."

There were murmurs of agreement here. Susie, who'd been in the National Guard, thumped the table.

The man waited for quiet before he continued: "There's no longer just one superpower in the world. And if we don't stamp down hard, and fast, the Chinese will be ahead of us. We're deep in a recession. We're losing jobs, companies, manufacturing capabilities, resources. America is bleeding to death, and no one in Washington gives a damn. They won't even lift a finger to get our boys back. That tells you everything."

He looked around, pleased to see the attentive faces. The men were nodding. The woman at the back of the room with the long, dark hair was watching him carefully. She looked impressed, and he liked that. She'd only been with them a few weeks, but she'd come highly recommended.

Even so, the man didn't trust her. Until they proved themselves, really proved themselves, he trusted no one. It was a philosophy that had kept him alive and out of prison. But even without that, there was something about the woman that made him uneasy. He'd definitely be keeping a close eye on her in the hours ahead…

"The fight back starts here, and it starts now. You know that," the man went on. "But like I said – I lied. We've been training for weeks now for this mission. And you think our target is that weak-brained Senator O'Donnaldson-Smythe. Hell, even his name screams 'liberal', don't it? Yet he backs China against the freedom fighters in Wiengwei, the heroic rebels who've been so supportive of our cause, our fight against the Red Death."

"So, if it ain't the Senator…?" Hank from Tennessee asked.

"Nope, not the Senator. He can have his little party tomorrow in peace and quiet and never know how close he came to being a hostage in his own home. We have a new target, ladies and gentlemen. The floor plans and schematics you've all learned are not the Senator's house. They're not quite the place we're really going either, in case that gave things away. I have new ones for you to look at now, but you'll find they're actually very similar. We've been planning this for a while. And now we're going after a bigger, even more dangerous fish, my friends."

Jefferson Kent straightened up and folded his arms. He looked round the table, making eye contact with everyone in turn. Especially the woman at the back.

When the tension was so thick you could cut it, Jefferson Kent told them what they were going to do. What they'd *really* been training for. And he was pleased to see that even the dark-haired woman's eyes widened and her face paled with shock.

7

The huge lorries of the Chinese army convoy looked like tiny toys as they snaked their way along the narrow, twisting road through the valley.

It had taken Chance and Mr Chang a whole day to find the warheads. Mr Chang had left Yoshi with his sister, before he and Chance checked each of the several possible routes back to safer Chinese territory. Now they watched through binoculars from the top of one of the high cliffs overlooking the road.

"Not far now," said Mr Chang. "Another few hours and they will be out of the more dangerous areas where the rebels still operate, and back in safer Chinese territory."

"I hope they aren't getting complacent because of that," Chance told him.

"They look well guarded."

There were trucks full of Chinese troops between the three large lorries. What the lorries carried was hidden under huge tarpaulins stretched over their cargo, but Chance was sure it had to be the warheads. What else could it be – the size and the number was about right, and the heavy guard contingent meant it was important. The fact it was material heading out of Wiengwei and away from the conflict zone was another indication. Most Chinese military supplies were being brought *into* the war zone.

"So what do we do now?" Mr Chang asked.

"We watch. Make sure they make it home. With luck we won't have to do any more than that."

Mr Chang nodded. "We should move on."

They headed back to Mr Chang's car, parked far back from the edge of the cliff so as to be well out of sight from below. There was a narrow track along the cliff top. Further on, according to Mr Chang's map, it zig-zagged down to meet the road at the valley floor. But the track was too narrow and too steep for the military vehicles. Chance hoped it wouldn't turn out to be too narrow or steep for the car. If it started – they should have left it running, he thought.

The engine protested, but caught on the third attempt. The car belched black exhaust fumes into the afternoon, before lurching unevenly along the rough track.

The explosion was so powerful it shook the car. Mr Chang braked hard and the car skidded to a halt in a cloud of pale dust.

Chance was out of the vehicle even before it had stopped. He ran to the edge of the cliff, dropping to the ground as he neared the edge. Then he crawled the last few metres and peered over, down into the valley.

The lead truck was on fire and strips of canvas floated down through the air. The road was blocked with the charred, burning shell of the vehicle. Men were shouting, running. The flatbed lorry at the back of the convoy was trying to reverse, its trailer slewing across the road.

"Landmine?" Mr Chang asked, joining Chance.

Chance shook his head. "No crater. And the main damage is at the top of the truck. Rocket-propelled grenade more likely."

"Which means the rebels are here."

Chance pointed across the valley. There was a flash from behind one of the bushes that grew sparsely on the steep banks. "You got those binoculars handy?"

"Surely they will detonate the warheads if they destroy the trucks," said Mr Chang. "We should get away from here, fast."

Chance shook his head. "The warheads will survive the explosions and fire. They need to be primed and activated to go off. Which is good news because I doubt if your car can outrun a nuclear explosion!"

"A good point," Mr Chang conceded, handing Chance the binoculars.

The other side of the valley was suddenly alive with flashes of gunfire. Chinese soldiers dived for better cover. Several were hit in the first volleys and fell to the ground. Chance could hear the commander shouting orders as the Chinese soldiers returned fire. But the rebels were well dug in, and the convoy was a sitting target.

The lorry in the middle of the convoy lurched forwards, smashing into the burning remains of the lead truck. For a moment it looked as though the flatbed lorry would push the truck aside and clear a path for the convoy to escape.

But then there was a streak of flame from high on the side of the valley.

"Incoming," Chance muttered.

The missile hit the side of the cab and the whole front

of the flatbed lorry exploded into fragments. The blast twisted the trailer round and tipped it on its side. There was no way the convoy could advance now.

Then a second later, the truck at the back of the convoy exploded. The remaining lorries and a number of soldiers were trapped between the burning vehicles.

"Tell me," said Chance to Mr Chang, "have you ever heard of the Seventh Cavalry?"

"Anything to do with Custer's Last Stand?" Mr Chang asked.

"That's the one. We'd better see what we can do to help."

They ran back to Mr Chang's car. The engine was still running, and Chance got into the driver's seat. Mr Chang frowned, but said nothing.

As the car pulled away, Mr Chang asked, "Why didn't they destroy all the vehicles?"

"They need to keep one flatbed lorry intact to drive a warhead or two away. The Chinese commander will have called in air support. They're on a schedule now and they're running out of time. They have an hour if they're lucky."

"So, we have to slow them down until help arrives."

"Exactly."

"How do we do that? What's the plan?"

Chance was concentrating on the road as they raced along the narrow track. "Ask me in an hour."

Ahead, the track turned and dipped over the edge of the cliff. It was a point where vehicles needed to slow and edge cautiously down the steep slope.

Chance changed down a gear, then floored the accelerator.

The car leaped forward, the sound of its engine deepening. The track disappeared from view for a moment as the car left the ground. Then it slammed down, and the track was twisting ahead of them. Chance spun the wheel, slewing the car into the first tight bend, then back the other way into the next hairpin.

They were bouncing and sliding. The car missed one of the bends completely and careered on down the slope to rejoin the track at the next tight turn. Dislodged stones and rocks scattered and rolled ahead of them. A bullet cracked into the windscreen as they approached the convoy – though whether it had been fired by the Chinese troops or the rebels it was impossible to tell.

The glass crazed, and Chance shoved it away with the flat of his hand, knocking a large hole in the windshield. The car finally skidded to a halt beside the burning cab of the front flatbed lorry. It stalled.

Chance's door was jammed shut, bent out of shape where it had skimmed the side of the lorry. He clambered quickly across and out the other side, following Mr Chang.

"Tell them to hold their position," Chance yelled at Mr Chang. "Tell them they just have to hold out till help arrives. Keep under cover and hold off the rebels."

One of the Chinese soldiers was shouting back at them. The man dashed across to the shelter of the wrecked lorry.

"He says he's in charge and wants to know who we are," Mr Chang told Chance.

"Tell him we were just passing and thought they could use some help."

Mr Chang spoke to the commander, who stared back at him for a moment in disbelief. Then he laughed, and spoke rapidly in reply.

"He doesn't believe me, but he says he can tell we aren't rebels because we have a sense of humour."

"Guess he won't have us shot then."

The commander laughed again as Mr Chang translated. But his humour did not last. The rebels were coming down the valley side, picking their way closer, running from one area of cover to the next.

"We have to stop them getting the warheads," Chance shouted above the increasing gunfire. "Just one of them is enough to devastate a major city."

Mr Chang shook his head as he passed that on and the commander replied. "He says that even though we are worryingly well-informed about his cargo, we must think he is stupid. They knew a long time ago the rebels were after the warheads, and prepared for the eventuality."

"What do you mean?" Chance ducked as a bullet pinged off the broken metal close to his head. "Aren't the warheads on these trucks?"

"Yes," said Mr Chang, translating. "The warheads are too valuable to abandon unless they have to. But all the nuclear material was all removed and flown back to Beijing weeks ago."

It was Chance's turn to laugh. "Then what are we waiting for? If these are off the DK 5s we saw, the warheads have a remote trigger. We can set them to think they're about to impact, and they'll explode. If we build in a delay, we can get away and leave the warheads here to detonate when the rebels arrive at the trucks."

The commander frowned as Mr Chang passed that on. He pulled out a radio and started shouting urgently into it.

"He didn't know that," Mr Chang told Chance. "He's trying to find an engineer."

"Who needs an engineer?" said Chance. "Come on!"

Ignoring the shouted protests of the Chinese commander, Chance hauled himself up on to the flatbed trailer. The tarpaulin was scarred and burned, but intact. Chance pulled out a large hunting knife from a holster on his belt and sliced though the heavy material. Then he pushed his way inside.

There was just enough light to see. The warheads were still fitted within the nose cones of the missiles; it was as if they had just been sheared off. Using the tip of his knife, Chance quickly undid a locking screw and eased open an inspection cover. Behind it was a small display screen and a series of switches. They were labelled with Chinese characters.

"Mr Chang!" Chance yelled. "I'm going to need some language help here."

Chance pointed to switches, asking what they were. Then he began to work.

"It will take forever to set each warhead," said Mr Chang as Chance closed the final switch in the sequence. The display flashed up '180', which became '179', then '178'.

"Don't need to. One per load will do it."

"Even so, how long will that take?"

"Now I've worked out the sequence? Shouldn't be more than a couple of minutes."

The hardest part was getting to the last lorry. The rebels were almost on them. The Chinese commander ordered his men to give Chance covering fire, and he disappeared into the dark space beneath the tarpaulin. A few seconds later he was out again.

"I set that one for less than one minute," he shouted. "Time to retreat."

"Well past time," Mr Chang yelled back as together with the surviving soldiers they ran back towards the remains of the lead vehicles. "I estimate thirty seconds till the first one blows."

"Better take the car then."

Chance leaped through the open passenger door of Mr Chang's car, flinging himself across to the driver's seat. The commander was shouting orders to his men, and several of them piled into the back of Chang's car. More clung to the sides and the open back doors. Bullets rattled off the back of the car – catching one of the soldiers who twisted and fell away with a cry.

Chance turned the key in the ignition. The engine

caught first time and roared into life.

"Hey," said Mr Chang, "I think you fixed it!"

Then the car screeched away. Smaller than the military vehicles, there was just enough room for it to get past the burning remains of the front lorry. Chance accelerated away. In the cracked rear-view mirror he could see the rebels swarming over the flatbeds, waving their guns in triumph.

Then the warheads exploded in sequence. The first one that Chance had set went first. The massive blast set off the others in the same load, and the valley was filled with flame and smoke. Chance could feel the heat of it as the shockwave bounced the car forwards down the valley.

Then the second flatbed lorry exploded. The third went off almost simultaneously and a huge ball of fire filled the sky. Black smoke billowed up, blotting out the valley walls.

The Chinese commander leaned into the car and spoke to Mr Chang.

"He says we can leave him and his men here and they will wait for the air support. He thinks they will find him easily now."

"He's not wrong," Chance agreed.

"He says the rebels will not be happy now that, how do

you say it? The birds have flown."

Chance laughed. "That's true too."

Then his laughter died away as he remembered what Ralph had said to Rich. "If the birds have flown, they will try for the Football." He slammed his fists into the steering wheel in anger. "That's what he meant. Of course. And I'm probably too late to stop it now."

"What are you talking about, my friend?"

"Forget a few disarmed nuclear warheads," Chance told him. "If the Wiengwei rebels have a plan to get the Football, then the whole world is in danger!"

8

The morning of the reception, Chuck White arranged for Rich, Jade and Dex Halford to get a private tour of the White House. It was pretty much the same tour as most visitors got, but for just the three of them.

The tour only covered the main, central building – the Executive Residence or Mansion House, as it was called. Chuck promised to show them the West Wing, where the President and his staff actually worked, after lunch.

Although she knew that the rooms they were seeing had been decorated and presented deliberately to be impressive, Jade was awestruck. Even the visitors' foyer left her breathless. And wherever she went, she was conscious that this was *the* White House – one of the most famous buildings in the world. And home to one of the most powerful people in the world.

Unusually, Rich seemed just as impressed. He was uncharacteristically quiet as they were shown the Library, the Vermeil Room, the China Room, the Map Room, the Blue Room and the Red Room; they even had a quick tour of the kitchens.

Chuck took them out for lunch. They looked back at the huge building from the other side of Pennsylvania Avenue, and Jade found it hard to believe she'd been inside just minutes ago.

After lunch, Chuck promised them a quick tour of the famous West Wing. This was where the President's Oval Office overlooked the Rose Garden, and where the Cabinet Room and other offices were housed.

"Though it isn't really big enough any more," Chuck told them. "Most of the staff have spilled out into the Eisenhower Building just next door."

They started in the basement. Chuck told them this was where his own office was situated, as well as general administration, the rest rooms, canteen, a few conference rooms and the Situation Room.

"Lucky there isn't a situation today," said Dex, as Chuck showed them inside.

Even so, there were several people in business suits

working away on laptops at the long conference table. Flat-panel displays were fixed to the walls, and there was a bank of telephones.

"Secure communications and heavy duty shielding," said Chuck. "Better leave these guys to it. They keep a constant watch on what's going on in the world, gathering data from a multitude of sources, always on the lookout for trouble."

"And do they find it?" Jade asked.

Chuck grinned. "Sometimes. Thanks, guys," he called as he ushered them out again.

"Is that the most secret and secure room in the White House, then?" Rich asked.

"Guess so. Except maybe…" Chuck shrugged. "Yeah, probably." He gave a knowing, teasing smile.

"Oh come on," Rich told him. "You can't leave it at that."

"Promise not to tell anyone, and I'll show you what's really the most secure and secret room. Though with everyone demanding freedom of information, the word 'secret' doesn't mean what it once did."

Chuck led them back along a corridor to where he had pointed out the main Secret Service office. It was a large open-plan room with partitioned workspaces. In fact, it was boringly like any other office.

But before they reached it, they passed another smaller room, and a narrow flight of stairs. The stairs jutted out into the corridor, the side was faced with dark, wooden panels.

"These come out near the Press Secretary's office and the Cabinet Room," said Chuck. "We'll go up there in a minute."

"And is this the room?" Rich asked, sounding slightly awed. He pointed to the door closest to the stairs.

Chuck White laughed. "We have everything here in the White House. It's like a big village. Self-sufficient. And that," he went on, lowering his voice to a conspiratorial whisper, "is the barber's shop."

Without waiting for a reaction, Chuck pushed open the door and led the way inside. It looked just like an ordinary office – with oak-panelled walls and a large wooden desk.

"No one in today, but this is now the Office of Homeland Security," said Chuck. "The barber was evicted a few years ago. Now he makes house calls."

It was the first room in the West Wing that hadn't been a hive of activity. Jade was surprised how many people there were – even in the corridors.

"Is that what you were going to show us?" Jade asked. "An empty room?" It seemed to her that Chuck had been heading past this room when Rich had asked about it.

"Of course."

"Really?" Halford asked.

"How can you doubt me?" Chuck shook his head. "OK, you got me," he admitted. "The most secret room in the White House is actually the cupboard under these stairs."

Without further explanation, Chuck led them up the nearby stairs to the first floor. In fact, it was also the ground floor as the West Wing was built into the hill side. So at the back of the building, the President's Oval Office, although on this upper floor, had a view out over the grounds and a door out into the famous Rose Garden.

Chuck gave them a quick look at the Roosevelt Room, which was where they would later be meeting the President. It was a large room, almost square but with a corner flattened off and a door set at an angle across. There were two other doors, and a large conference table in the middle of the room. There was a large fireplace on one wall, several paintings, and a grandfather clock.

"Which Roosevelt is it named after – Theodore or Franklin D?" Halford asked.

"Both really," said Chuck. "Theodore had the room built, and FDR expanded it. So Nixon named it after them. Seems fair enough. Franklin D. Roosevelt used to keep fish in here."

"I'd have thought receptions like this would be in the main house, the Residence," said Halford.

"Usually, yes. But this is rather less formal. Less public. Just you guys and few other dignitaries. A couple of guys from the Chinese Embassy who have a meeting with the President beforehand are staying too. So the President thought he'd meet and greet close to his office and away from the public. Saves him the walk as well."

"Do we get to see the Oval Office?" Rich asked.

"Maybe later. Ask the President, he'll probably be happy to show you the Oval Office. And the Cabinet Room – that's through from his secretary who has an office adjoining the President's."

"Can't we see it now?" Jade asked. "Just a quick look?"

Chuck shook his head. "Afraid not. The President's working in there."

"At least show us where it is," Rich begged.

Chuck laughed. "It's just through here. This place isn't nearly as big as people imagine, you know."

He led them out of the door set at an angle. Now Rich

could see it was angled because the corridor outside was cutting across what would otherwise be the corner of the room.

"The Oval Office," said Chuck quietly, pointing across the corridor to a large wooden door just a short distance away.

There was a man in a dark suit sitting on an upright chair outside the door. He nodded at Chuck. "How you doing, sir?"

"Pretty good, thanks, Steve."

Steve was cradling a briefcase on his lap. It was made of metal, and Rich could see that it was attached to the man's wrist by a thick, metal chain.

"Nice case," said Rich. "Something important?"

"You could say that," Steve replied. He glanced at Chuck, who nodded.

"He'll guess anyway. He's a bright kid," said Chuck.

"Today, I'm the Bagman," said Steve. "I keep close to the President at all times, and hope he never needs this." He tapped the briefcase with his free hand. "This is the briefcase that contains the nuclear launch codes and the equipment to send them."

Jade gasped. Halford nodded, obviously having guessed this already. Rich felt slightly queasy just at the thought of the powerful information inside the briefcase.

Chuck grinned, obviously used to living and working close to the instruments of Armageddon. "We call it the Football," he said.

9

The J-10 fighter was designed to be inherently aerodynamically unstable. The fly-by-wire systems compensated for that, and made use of it to make the aircraft even more manoeuvrable and agile. With its swept back delta wings, small front wings that pivoted under the cockpit and no tail fins, it was exactly what John Chance needed.

The problem was the Chinese People's Liberation Army Air Force was not going to let him have it.

The commander of the warhead convoy had been grateful to Chance and Mr Chang for their help preventing the warheads getting into rebel hands – even without their nuclear weapons they would have been powerful explosives. He was even more grateful to them for saving his life. So grateful he was very keen for Chance and Mr Chang to wait and meet his superior officers and explain who they were and how they happened to be in that part of Wiengwei at exactly the right time.

Chance told Mr Chang to agree enthusiastically as they sat waiting for the helicopters to arrive. Then as soon as they got the opportunity, they leaped back into Mr Chang's car – the engine still running – and sped away.

Now that Chance had realised what Ralph had been trying to tell Rich, he needed to get in touch with Ardman urgently. The rebels were after the Football – the American nuclear launch codes.

He couldn't risk telling the Chinese military that American nuclear launch capabilities might be compromised. They would quickly work out the first target of a nuke in the hands of the Wiengwei rebels might be Beijing, and launch a pre-emptive strike again the US. However dire the situation might be – and Chance really didn't know if there genuinely was a threat – he didn't fancy being responsible for starting World War Three.

For the same reason, he couldn't risk calling Ardman. If the call was intercepted, the consequences could be just as grave.

This meant Chance had to get out of China as quickly as possible – and that was why he and Mr Chang were parked outside the perimeter of the PLAAF airbase examining a squadron of J-10s through binoculars.

"Can you fly one of those?" Mr Chang asked.

"I'll have a go." Chance grinned. "Actually, I happen to know the cockpit design is a 'Hands-On-Throttle-And-Stick' set-up very similar to western fighters. It's been a while, but I think I'll manage."

"Even with the controls labelled in Chinese?"

"You're lucky it's a single-seater," said Chance. "If they had the two-seater trainer version there, you'd be coming with me."

"That might be safer than what you're suggesting."

The guards at the gate scrutinised the two passes that Mr Chang showed them. But they were used to surprise inspections, and let the two inspectors through. One of the guards called ahead to warn the base commander. If either of them noticed that only one of the inspectors spoke, while the other stood a short way off, his head down and his cap low over his eyes, they said nothing – intimidated perhaps by the man's powerful build.

The base commander was keen to help. He knew of

other bases where the commanding officer had been immediately replaced after a snap inspection. Or ended up running a refuelling depot in the middle of nowhere, or patrolling the northern borders with criminals and undesirables. Or out of a job altogether.

So when the chief inspector demanded to start by examining the state of the aircraft and their readiness for action, he agreed at once.

"And they are fuelled and ready to take off immediately?" Chang demanded.

"Of course, sir. Several of the planes are taken out of service briefly for maintenance or refuelling. But the others are prepared and can take off at a moment's notice."

"Your typical scramble time, from alert to airborne?"

The commander blustered. "The times are getting better and better, sir. We practise constantly."

"The exact times?"

"I shall have to check the records," the commander confessed.

Chang nodded. "Very well. But first, I think we shall inspect the state of the aircraft themselves. He turned to Chase. "You will examine the cockpit of that aircraft." He pointed to the nearest of the J-10s.

"Your colleague is actually going to check inside the plane?" The commander was sweating. He had never known this before. What was going on – was it a new, even tougher inspection? Had someone in Beijing already decided the base should fail?

"Helmet for my colleague, please," Chang demanded. "He will also be checking the head-up display settings."

The commander nodded to the engineers gathered round and listening. "Get him a flight helmet."

Steps were wheeled to the side of the plane. Chance turned away as he removed his cap to put on the heavy flight helmet and it occurred to the commander that he had not properly seen the tall man's face since he arrived, but he said nothing.

Then Chance climbed into the aircraft and strapped himself in.

"We shall of course be conducting a brief engine check," Chang announced.

It seemed to the base commander that the inspector was nervous too. And that made the commander even more wary. "I'm not sure I can allow that, sir," he said hesitantly, aware that his career was on the line. Should he object – was he *supposed* to object?

Chang nodded, as if pleased. At the same moment, the

massive AL-31FN turbofan engine – actually manufactured in Russia – burst into life. The sound drowned out whatever Chang was saying.

But the commander was no longer listening. He was watching in open-mouthed amazement as the J-10 started to move out on to the runway.

Chang smiled and held his hand up, shaking his head as if to say: "Don't worry."

The engineers were looking at the commander for instructions. Pilots were running to see what was happening. The plane started down the runway, engine sound deepening as it increased power.

The J-10 was designed to have a short take-off and to climb steeply and rapidly to its cruising altitude. It was only a matter of seconds before the plane was roaring into the sky high above the airbase.

The commander stared in horror at Chang. "What is going on?"

Chang met his gaze calmly. "You were right to question whether we should start the engines. Unfortunately, you were a little late in that realisation, which will not look so good on my report. But rest assured I will note your diligence and alertness. I do of course have the necessary paperwork and authorisation for the air trials my colleague is now performing."

He produced a sheaf of papers from his uniform jacket, but then stuffed them away again before the commander could take them.

"Which I shall show you when we go over my preliminary findings at the end of this inspection." He checked his watch. "The air trials will take about ninety minutes. I will see you in your office when my colleague returns and we shall discuss an appropriate action plan for the base – to be carried out under your continued command."

The commander tried not to look too relieved. "Thank you, sir."

"Assuming," Chang continued, "that I find the perimeter intact and properly patrolled. I will require transport so I can check this for myself. No driver, I shall go alone and make spot checks wherever I deem necessary."

"Of course, sir."

"And I will meet you in your office in, shall we say two hours?"

The commander nodded. "That will be most convenient."

Chang smiled. "I shouldn't really say this,

Commander, but judging by what I have seen so far, I think an 'A' rating will be a formality. The promotion board will be impressed. Congratulations."

The commander swallowed. "Promotion board?"

"Forget I said that. Something else we can discuss later perhaps."

On the way back to his office, the base commander was almost walking on air. A snap inspection with an 'A' rating, a promotion board... He sat at his desk staring into space, thinking about how his life might just have changed.

Which was why he didn't notice that Chang drove the Warrior – a clone of the US Jeep – straight to the main gate and out of the base. It would be almost three hours before he realised his life had indeed just changed, but not in the way he imagined...

High above the clouds, John Chance was impressed with the all-round visibility afforded by the two-piece bubble canopy. He took the J-10 to supersonic speed, and headed for the border with India.

He didn't imagine it would be easy getting there. The Indian Air Force would take some convincing that he wasn't starting an invasion, but at least they might understand English.

The Chinese could be more of a problem. The J-10 was designed in the 1990s and had been in service since 2004, but it has only been officially announced to the world late in 2006. Even now, its actual capabilities were a mystery. A mystery that would unravel as soon as Chance landed his stolen fighter on foreign soil. Once they realised what was happening, the PLAAF would shoot him down rather than let that happen.

Even at supersonic speed, it was going to be a long flight.

10

A white limousine arrived for them at six o'clock. Jade was wearing a pale blue dress; the hem was just shy of the floor, and that was with high heels. Rich looked smart but slightly uncomfortable in a dark suit and plain tie. Halford – as ever – looked as though he might have slept in his suit. He seemed totally relaxed, a contrast to Jade and Rich's palpable nervousness.

"The White House, yeah?" the uniformed driver checked, calling back through the sliding smoked-glass partition. He made it sound like any other destination.

"West Wing," Halford confirmed.

"Sure thing. You British? Love that accent."

"*I* don't have an accent," Halford told him, closing the partition.

Chuck White had arranged for them to arrive early so he could greet them in person. He was waiting for them when they arrived, wearing his dark suit. Rich could see the arm of his sunglasses poking out of his top pocket.

"On duty?" Rich asked.

"Sort of. Never off duty when I'm at the office, but I'm also a guest at the reception."

"Is that unusual?" Jade asked.

Chuck nodded. "The hired help doesn't usually get to stay for champagne."

"Quite an honour then," said Halford.

"Guess so."

The Roosevelt Room seemed much bigger without the conference table. There were several smaller tables against the walls, covered with white cloths. One had plates stacked at the end – each plate printed with the presidential seal.

Two uniformed waitresses were putting out food. A man in a dark grey suit was arranging chairs and music stands in the opposite corner of the room.

"Is there a band?" Rich asked.

"A small orchestra," Chuck told him. "We don't skimp on ceremony here, isn't that right, Chester?"

"They should be here by now," the man sorting out the

chairs said. "It's a new lot; they haven't been before. I'll just check they have the address." He smiled and rolled his eyes. Flipping open a mobile phone, his smile turned to a frown. "Funny – no signal. Still, the walk will do me good. I'll see if they're in the visitors' foyer."

More guests were arriving. The waitresses were offering champagne or orange juice, served from silver trays. Rich couldn't stop grinning, and he was pleased to see that Jade and Halford were also smiling.

"This is the life," said Halford. "Waitress service, as much champagne as you can drink. Bit of food and some sophisticated music later."

"And a chat with the President of the United States," said Jade.

"Maybe he'll give a speech," said Rich. "Tell some jokes."

"He was a navy pilot, not a stand-up comedian," said Halford with a laugh. "Your poor dad doesn't know what he's missing.

Rich felt his good mood fade.

Jade had stopped smiling. "I just hope he's all right."

"He'll be fine," Halford reassured her. "He won't let a few Chinese rebels and the odd nuclear missile slow him down for long."

Rich reckoned Halford was right. "Even so, it's a shame he's not here." Instinctively he checked his cell phone. Like Chester's it had no signal – typical.

"But we're glad you came," Jade was saying to Halford. "There's no one quite like Dad…" She hesitated, thinking about this. "Which is maybe a good thing," she decided. "But you're as close as anyone gets."

Halford laughed. "I think that's a compliment."

"Hey look, the band has arrived," said Rich.

"Orchestra," Jade corrected him.

There were maybe a dozen musicians, setting up their instruments and getting ready in the corner where the music stands and chairs were arranged.

One of the female musicians was wearing a plain, dark grey suit, her brown hair tied up. She turned away as Rich looked at her so he could only see the back of her head. But for just a moment he thought there was something familiar about her. He was sure he'd seen her somewhere before. Was she famous, maybe? Had he seen her on television, or the cover of a CD?

But then Chuck returned to tell them that the food was arriving and soon the President would join them, and Rich thought no more about it.

*

The first the Police Department knew about it was when the tanks rolled in. It was a strange sight – battle tanks on the streets of Washington DC. Even stranger to see them rumbling down Pennsylvania Avenue, past the White House.

The phone line for the Chief of Police was burning. Messages were piling up. The Mayor was threatening to come over in person. And still he couldn't get any response from the military.

"Can somebody tell me why there are goddamn tanks on the Avenue?" he bellowed.

Finally, with something close to relief on her face, his secretary told the Chief that a General Harris Wilson was on the line demanding to speak with him.

"Thank God," the Chief said, taking the handset. "General Wilson – what the hell's going on? Are we being invaded?"

"I think we've both been the victims of some serious miscommunication," the General's voice replied. He had a deep, southern accent. "And I can sure tell you I'll bite the hide off whoever screwed this up."

"What's going on?"

"Manoeuvres. A major anti-terrorism exercise. Been planned for nearly a year, and now they tell me that no one thought to inform you guys that we're sealing off the Avenue and other roads close to the White House for twenty-four hours. How can that happen, Chief? You tell me that."

How indeed, the Chief of Police wondered. His anxiety was giving way to relief, but he found he was angry too. "You can't just do that," he heard himself saying.

The General laughed. "Bit late to tell us now. Anyway, it was all cleared with Homeland Security, the Secret Service and the FBI. Hell, even the Fire Department got informed, yet some joker decides you guys don't need to know. The boys who keep this great capital city of ours running, and no one thinks to tell you? Jeez. I got to hand it to you, Chief, your guys do a great job. It's an honour and a privilege to be working with you all on this one. You give me a call if you need any further clarification, won't you? And I just know I can count on you if my team needs anything."

The Chief opened his mouth to tell the General he was sending a team over to monitor what was happening, and that in his city unless there was a war on he – the Chief of Police – was in charge of any law and order exercises.

But the phone was dead. General Wilson had hung up.

*

"All sorted, folks," General Wilson told the policemen standing by the container truck that was his operations suite. It was parked – or rather, stopped – in the middle of Pennsylvania Avenue. Behind it, the floodlit White House looked on impassively.

"What did the Chief say?" a police lieutenant asked.

"Like I told you, there's been a screw-up. All sorted now. Of course, you'd better call in and double check with the Chief's Office. Don't want you guys getting into trouble. And as soon as you've done that, Major Brandon has a road map showing where we need the cordons. No civilians inside, right? Not even the fearless boys in blue. You need anything – you stand at the line and holler."

The ground beneath them shook as an M1A2 main battle tank, weighing close to seventy tons, passed by. Its enormous 1500 horse power gas-turbine engine drowned out any protest the police lieutenant might have made.

The tank had been fitted with a TUSK – Tank Urban Survival Kit – which modified it specifically for warfare in an urban environment. Amongst other additions, this meant it had a remote-operated weapons-station mounted on top of the turret, and infra-red sighting. The machine gun, controlled from inside the tank, swivelled slowly to point across the grass towards the White House.

Jade got to the food before Rich, which, she thought to herself, meant there was still some left. There was plenty of vegetarian food for once, and she loaded her plate. A few minutes ago she had been too nervous to think about eating. Now she realised she was hungry.

She moved away from the buffet to let others take their turn. Nearby, the orchestra was still setting up. It seemed to be taking them a long time. She watched a young woman in a dark grey trouser suit unloading a cello from its large, black case. The cello slipped, and almost fell.

Instinctively, Jade moved to help. But the man beside the woman caught it easily and held it for her. He was very ordinary looking with short brown hair, but it was the woman who drew Jade's attention.

It was Kate Hunter – Chuck White's colleague – Jade was sure of it. But Chuck had told them Kate was away in New York State. How could she be here – and in the orchestra?

"Hi there," said Jade, smiling. "Didn't think I'd be seeing you."

The woman's expression froze and she glared at Jade. Giving the slightest shake of her head, she said: "I'm real sorry, but I don't think I know you."

Jade was about to protest, but there was something about the woman's tone. Something about the way she flicked her eyes quickly and urgently towards the brown-haired man beside her. Something about the way the man's very ordinary looking eyes narrowed and hardened as he waited for Jade to reply.

"I'm sorry," said Jade. "I just meant, I'm surprised to see an orchestra. It's going to be some party." She forced a smile.

The brown-haired man smiled back. "One hell of a party," he said. His voice was a husky whisper. "You can bet on that, young lady."

Jade turned and moved quickly away. She didn't know who the man was, though his whole demeanour had unsettled her. But she was certain that despite her protestations, the woman was Kate Hunter, agent of the US Secret Service.

11

There were two Chinese fighters on Chance's tail. He had them on radar, but since they were J-10s exactly like he was flying, they couldn't catch him up. He just had to hope they couldn't get within missile range.

He was almost at the border with India, but whether the Chinese planes would turn back remained to be seen. If there was no sign of the Indian Air Force, they might risk following him.

Chance was running low on fuel, and keeping the plane at supersonic speed was draining the tanks even quicker, but he didn't have much choice. If he slowed down, he'd be dead. If he didn't, the plane would run out of fuel and crash.

Just as he reckoned he was reaching the point where he

would have to decide whether he wanted to be shot down or fall out of the sky – either inside a crashing plane or on an ejector seat - the fighters behind him turned away. Chance double-checked the radar. They were definitely breaking off. But why? What were they planning? What did they know that he didn't?

Chance soon found out. Four more planes were approaching him rapidly from in front. Somehow the Chinese had managed to get fighters ahead of him. He was going too fast to avoid them, the ambush was perfect.

"Running out of options," Chance muttered. If he opened fire first, he could start a small war. Maybe even a big one. If he didn't, and they got missile lock...

But the fighters didn't seem to be attacking. They had slowed and were approaching cautiously. He could see the first of them ahead – an elongated, ungainly dark grey shape against the blue of the sky. It looked more like a Russian design than Chinese.

As the plane banked and manoeuvred to come alongside, Chance saw the Indian Air Force markings. He reduced speed. The pilot of the other plane was pointing and gesturing, clearly wanting Chance to follow him. On the radar, Chance could see that the other three Indian planes were holding their positions – ready to attack if

Chance tried anything. He gave the Indian pilot a thumbs-up, hoping to show he was friendly.

He had crossed the border and not even realised. When they were further into Indian air space, the other planes joined the formation. Jointly built by India and Russia, the SU-30MKIs kept Chance's Chinese J-10 hemmed in as they escorted it to their base.

It was the early hours of the morning when Ardman took the call. He was reading a detective novel, which he was pretty sure he'd solved in chapter four, and sipping from a large glass of single malt whisky.

"Let me see if I've understood this correctly," he said, swirling the amber liquid round the glass and letting the ice cubes clink together. "You are with the commander of an Indian airbase, and he's happy to let you use his secure line, and to arrange transport, despite the fact you violated Indian air space without any identification or authorisation, if I get the Foreign Secretary to vouch for you."

"And in return for a second-hand Chinese J-10," Chance replied.

"Yes, well, I think we'll pretend I don't know about the theft of a secret fighter plane from the People's Liberation

Army Air Force for now. And we won't mention it to the Foreign Secretary either, thank you very much. Let's concentrate on your theory that the Wiengwei rebels are planning to get hold of US nuclear launch codes, shall we?"

"I have to get to Washington."

"And your new friends in India can arrange this for you, can they?"

"Near enough. In return for the plane."

Ardman sighed. "I suppose that will have to do then. But we want pictures and a copy of their technical report. Even if that means you have to go economy class."

"I do think speed might be of the essence."

Ardman had to agree. "I'll get the Foreign Office to make the necessary arrangements. And I'll check on your friend Ralph as well. Stay where you are for now, and I'll call you back in ten minutes."

"I'll look forward to it."

"Oh, and John…" Ardman began, "…well done." But Chance had hung up.

An hour later, Chance was on an Indian Air Force plane to an American base in Northern Iraq. A US Air Force jet was waiting there to fly him to Washington.

"So the Americans are on the case?" Chance asked Ardman as he called in between the flights.

"They claim they are. My contact at the Pentagon said they don't really believe there's any danger, but they had already got a threat warning in place. They don't take any risks where the President is concerned, and they know Marshal Wieng has considerable influence and resources. The Pentagon has already deployed special forces outside the White House in case of a full attack."

"They *are* taking it seriously," Chance agreed. "Just as well. From what I can gather from Mr Chang, Ralph was buying arms from some crooks in the Chinese military and selling them on to the rebels in Wiengwei. He would learn what he could of the rebel plans and targets and sell that information back to the Chinese government. But the Chinese found he was playing both sides, so when he discovered the nuclear plot he couldn't go back to them."

"So he went looking for the only other person he reckoned might listen to him – you. Even Ralph didn't fancy getting caught in the middle of a nuclear exchange," Ardman agreed. The Americans have General Wilson in charge. You'll liaise with him when you arrive. He shouldn't need much convincing, my friends tell me that it was his decision to up the threat level and deploy the troops."

"Sounds like they can handle it. It's good that they're prepared for anything."

There was a slight pause at the other end of the line. "Maybe a little too prepared. I've taken the precaution of sending some people to keep you company. Old friends and colleagues of yours, from Hereford."

"Understood."

"You'll find General Wilson parked somewhere on Pennsylvania Avenue."

Chance's plane was ready. His mind was already working through the possibilities as he climbed into the co-pilot's seat. He hoped that Jade and Rich – and Dex Halford – were all right. Normally, he wouldn't have worried at all. Inside the White House, they would be in one of the best protected buildings anywhere on the planet. The chances that anything could happen to them inside were minimal.

Ardman was naturally cautious, but even so, he must be more than usually suspicious to arrange for a team from Hereford to travel to Washington DC in secret – and it would *have* to be in secret. Because a facility near the market town of Hereford was the main base for the most efficient and deadly military special forces team in the world: the SAS.

The President was due in a few minutes. There was a heightened atmosphere at the reception as everyone waited. Conversations seemed hushed; there was a tangible sense of anticipation.

Jade had left the musicians as they unpacked and assembled their instruments. She had no idea what Kate Hunter was up to, but she wanted to find Chuck White. A dark-suited Secret Service agent accompanied several of the musicians from the room. A woman with flame red hair was carrying a long, black case.

"You take your flute to the bathroom?" the Secret Service man asked.

"I take it everywhere. You have no idea what a good flute costs these days."

Chuck was on the far side of the room. Jade could see him over the shoulders of several other people. Close to Chuck, she saw Dex Halford, and guessed Rich was there too.

Sure enough, as she approached, she caught sight of her brother's distinctive blond hair.

"Have you tried these sesame toast things?" Rich asked as Jade reached them.

"I haven't tried anything," Jade realised, glancing down at her plate. "I saw Kate Hunter."

"Thought she was out of town," said Halford. "That's what Chuck told us."

"She's with the orchestra." Jade was trying to attract Chuck's attention, but he seemed distracted. He held his hand up, gesturing for her to wait a moment. With his other hand he was adjusting his earpiece. A thin coiled wire ran down behind his ear and disappeared under his collar.

"Useless thing," Chuck muttered.

He looked round, trying to catch the eye of another Secret Service agent. The agent by the nearby door was also fiddling with his earpiece. Across the room, Jade saw another man trying to catch Chuck's eye. The agent raised his hands in a "what's up?" gesture and pointed to his own ear.

"I don't like this," said Chuck. "You guys stay here."

"My mobile's given up working too," said Rich. "No signal at all."

"Is it to do with Kate?" Jade asked.

"What?"

"Kate Hunter – she's with the orchestra."

Chuck froze. "Kate's here?"

Jade nodded, surprised at the sudden anxiety in the man's tone.

"Oh, my God," said Chuck. He raised his hand so he could speak quietly but urgently into the tiny microphone in the cuff of his jacket. "Can anyone hear me? Anyone got comms? This is Agent White declaring a situation. We have a Code Red, repeat Code Red. Do not bring in the President. Get him to a safe area now."

The agent on the other side of the room was still shrugging and tapping his ear. The man by the door didn't move.

There was an audible gasp as the door opened, and the President of the United States stepped into the room.

The ceramic gun is a myth. There is no firearm available that is made of a substance undetectable by x-ray scanners or metal detectors. The materials that might be used are simply not strong enough. And even if they were, the ammunition would be detected.

But there are other ways of getting a weapon past security checks. It was a compromise, but Jefferson Kent's team was willing to sacrifice speed for surprise. It took Kent himself several minutes to assemble his handgun from the metal components of the trumpet he had openly and legitimately brought through metal detectors and thorough searches into the White House.

The barrel was disguised as the trumpet's lead pipe. The stock was the tuning slide. The valves formed the handle and the magazine – bullets and tranquiliser darts had been concealed in lead sheaths within the valve casings.

The other weapons were just as ingeniously disguised. If everything went to plan – and Kent had no doubt that it would – then Lorraine Metz would have removed the knife concealed in the metal side of her flute case and killed the Secret Service agent escorting her, Hank and Tom to the restrooms. Hank had already quickly assembled his own handgun from a saxophone. Tom would take the agent's weapon. Then they would make their way to the Situation Room in the basement.

With all communications into and out of the West Wing already jammed, Jefferson Kent's next task was easy.

As the President stepped into the Roosevelt Room, Kent raised the fully assembled handgun and fired.

12

The sound of the single shot echoed round the room. Plaster fell from the ceiling where the bullet impacted.

Chuck White was already moving. As soon as the President appeared, he hurled himself towards the door with a shout of warning. His cry was lost in the noise and confusion.

The members of the orchestra were taking up position around the room, aiming their peculiar, but obviously deadly, handguns. Secret Service agents were drawing their own guns, but they were caught unawares, and there were too few of them in the room.

Rich saw Steve – the agent with the metal briefcase chained to his wrist – in the corridor behind the President. With his free hand he was drawing his gun. The first shot caught him in the shoulder and spun him round. A second slammed him to the ground.

The agent standing with the President reacted immediately. He grabbed the President's shoulders and dragged him back and down, pushing him out of the room. He turned so that his own body shielded his President. Chuck White was there too, dragging them both clear.

They almost made it.

Then two shots tore into the agent's back and he crashed to the floor. But the President was still moving. Chuck White dragged him out into the corridor. Two more agents appeared from the crowd of guests, shielding the President's escape and returning fire.

Rich felt himself grabbed from behind. He gave a yell of surprise, then realised it was Dex Halford. Dex gathered Jade with his other arm, and the three of them ran.

There was noise and confusion. Gunshots and shouts. A bullet kicked up close to Rich's foot as he reached the door.

Out into the corridor, the President, Chuck, and the other two agents were just in front of them. They were heading for the Oval Office on the other side of the wide corridor.

The Oval Office door was suddenly peppered with gunshots. Chuck dragged the President the other way.

A large man with a dark beard was charging down the corridor, firing as he came.

"He's got one of our guns," one of the agents yelled as they all backed away. A moment later, he was knocked sideways as a bullet caught him in the leg and he fell heavily against the wall.

Halford dragged Rich and Jade to the floor. Rich landed beside Steve – the man's eyes were closed, his face slack. The metal briefcase was inches from Rich's face, but still cuffed to Steve's wrist.

The attacker ducked into a doorway as Chuck returned fire.

"Get the cell phone!" Chuck was yelling. "Get Steve's cell phone."

"The phones aren't working," Rich yelled back.

"Just get it!"

He could see the agent's cell phone poking out of his inside jacket pocket. It was big – a combined phone and Personal Digital Assistant like a Blackberry or an iPhone – and it caught in the lining as he tried to grab it.

Jade and Halford ran to join Chuck, the President and the other surviving agent. Rich was still tugging at the phone. It was seriously bulky with a full QWERTY keyboard and LCD display. Finally, it came free and Rich was up and running after Jade and the others.

But the gunman was firing after them again. Another man from the orchestra had reached the doorway to the Roosevelt Room and was also firing.

"Get the President!" someone was shouting. "We need the President. And the codes!"

Jade disappeared round the corner of the corridor. She turned, staring back at Rich.

"Go!" he yelled.

A bullet tore into the wall close to his head. He dived sideways through the nearest doorway – a waiting room with sofa and armchairs. He slipped, fell, rolled across the floor and managed to crawl behind a sofa.

A split second later, the man with the dark beard appeared in the doorway. He glanced round the apparently empty room. "I know you're in here," he growled. "And there's no other way out."

The gunman saw the movement out of the corner of his eye. He turned and fired instinctively at the shape emerging from behind the sofa. His aim was deadly accurate.

*

Jefferson Kent swept plates and cutlery from the side table. One of the gunmen dragged Steve's body into the room and dumped him in a chair beside the table. The metal briefcase, still attached to Steve's wrist, was placed carefully on the table. "Wish we'd waited till he woke up," the gunman grumbled.

"Hey," another told him, "you're lucky he's not dead. He took a couple of the trank darts meant for the President. He'll be out for quite a while."

"We have the two Chinese delegates and some other impressive VIPs. Now we just need the man himself," said Kent.

"Tom's on it."

Kent turned to Kate Hunter, standing beside him. "I didn't see you shoot anyone."

"I thought the idea was to take hostages, not kill people," she told him.

"I guess it was. Let's get these hostages split up a bit. Lorraine will have us sealed in nice as pie, and it won't be long before the predictable General Wilson sends in the cavalry."

"You won't get away with this," shouted a Secret Service agent being held at gunpoint.

"Shut him up," said Kent, without turning.

The nearest gunman thumped the man viciously in the stomach. He doubled over, retching.

"Next time, it will be a bullet," Kent told him.

One of the gunmen handed Kent a handgun taken from a dead agent. Kent weighed it in his hand for a moment. Then he tossed away his own gun – a strange thing made from the pieces of a trumpet. It landed in a large bowl of fruit punch, splashing viscous liquid across the table.

"She doesn't get one," said Kent, waving his new handgun at Kate Hunter. "Not sure I trust you yet, new girl. You got to prove yourself."

"Let me have a gun, and I will."

Kent smiled. His hoarse whispering voice was the only sound in the room. "That's what worries me. Maybe that kid did recognise you. Maybe we'll keep an eye on you for a while, new girl." He turned away. "Now where the hell is the President?"

Halford grabbed Jade as she tried to run back.

"But – Rich!"

"Leave him. He'll have to look after himself."

Halford pulled Jade after him – following the President, Chuck and the other agent. Chuck led them through a conference room and out into an adjoining office. A Secret Service agent lay dead on the floor. His holster was empty.

"Where are we going?" the President demanded. "Who are these people? We have to make a stand."

"Too dangerous, Mr President," Chuck told him. "Believe me, these people mean business. We can't get to the Oval Office, so we're taking you to the Secure Area by the Chief of Staff's office. Then we can sit this out."

"Sit it out?" the President echoed in disbelief. "We need to take the fight to the enemy, Agent White. That's your job."

"My job is to keep you safe at all costs, Mr President. We can discuss what else is possible once we have reached the Secure Area."

The President nodded. "Very well."

"Dex – you and Jade stick with the President. I'll take the lead; Agent Harris will guard the rear. Any questions?"

As soon as he threw the cushion, Rich was up and running.

He had grabbed the cushion off the sofa as he crawled behind it. He hurled it along the back of the sofa, so it appeared at the far end. As Rich had hoped, the gunman turned and fired at the sudden movement.

Rich hurled himself forward from the other end of the sofa. He was across the small room before the gunman could turn. His shoulder collided with the man's arm, making his second shot go wide. A mirror on the wall exploded, as the gunman overbalanced and fell. Rich kicked out as hard as he could. He felt his foot connect with the man's wrist. The gun skidded away.

But Rich had no time to grab it. He wasn't sure he'd know what to do with it anyway – even if he could bring himself to shoot someone. He leaped over the fallen gunman and slammed the door closed behind him. There was no key or bolt, but at least the gunman couldn't see which way he went. In fact, he darted into a room on the opposite side of the corridor. Leaving the door open, he pressed himself back against the wall, out of sight.

Moments later, Rich heard the door opposite open. He guessed the gunman was trying to work out where Rich had gone, and whether it was worth trying to find him. After a few seconds hesitation, he heard heavy footsteps and a shadow passed across the doorway. Rich waited a full minute, then peered cautiously out into the corridor. It was empty.

He had no idea where Jade and the others were headed.

The only place that Rich could think of where he'd get help was the Situation Room in the basement. There had been agents there – surveillance screens too. They must have seen everything and would be preparing to counter attack. That had to be where Chuck White was taking the President.

Rich headed quickly and quietly in the direction he guessed – and hoped – would take him back to the stairs down to the basement.

Somewhere in the distance he could hear gunfire. He passed the body of a Secret Service woman lying face down. Her gun was gone. He crept past open doorways, alert and scared. Finally, he found the stairs where he and Jade and the others had come up from the basement. It seemed like days since he had been here, not just a couple of hours.

The basement was quiet and seemed deserted as he walked cautiously down the stairs. At the bottom, the door to the Secret Service offices was standing open. It had been ripped apart by gunfire. Rich glanced inside, then quickly looked away. There was no help to be had there.

Along the corridor, Rich moved past another dead body – a woman lying face down close to the side of the stairs. The back of her blouse was stained red. Rich swallowed and moved on quickly. He turned the corner to the Situation Room. At last, Rich could hear voices. There was someone still alive. He could practically taste the relief in his dry mouth.

Then he caught a glimpse of red hair. He recognised the profile of one of the women from the orchestra. She was standing in the doorway of the Situation Room, talking to a man. Beyond them, Rich could see the flat-screen monitors showing views of the outside of the White House and several corridors and rooms inside the building. On one screen, guests from the reception party were being led into a room, hands on their heads, by two gunmen.

There were several bodies, slumped in chairs and lying across the table.

Rich backed slowly away.

"Tell Kent we've initiated a complete lock-down," the woman was saying. "This place is so secure it makes Fort Knox look like open house on a cattle ranch. All the entrances, exits, windows and doors are sealed and they can only be unlocked from here. No one's coming in, and no one's getting out. Not even the President of the United States of America."

They both laughed.

Rich didn't think it was at all funny. He was trapped in the West Wing of the White House with a group of homicidal gunmen, alone and with nowhere to hide.

13

Rich watched from the corridor as the attackers in the Situation Room finished their conversation. The man strode from the room – on his way to report to Kent, as the woman had asked.

Rich was backing away, but now he had to hurry if he was going to avoid being seen. He turned and ran, desperately trying to keep quiet while moving as fast as he could.

He made it to the turn in the corridor; but behind him Rich could hear the man's heavy footsteps. The next section of corridor was longer. Could he get into one of the offices without making any noise? Would he be quick enough?

Ahead of him, Rich caught another glimpse of the

carnage in the Secret Service offices. No way was he hiding in there…

He glanced at the body of the woman. She was face down, one hand reaching out. Her legs were bent as if she had been running. But that couldn't be right, because she must have had her back to the side of the staircase. There was nowhere she could have been running *from*.

Then a shadow appeared at the top of the stairway, and Rich realised that someone was coming down. He was trapped between the man following him down the corridor, and the person coming down the stairs – killers in dinner suits with guns looted from dead agents.

His only chance was to get back down the stairs and into the Secret Service office after all. Except that now the approaching gunman would see Rich framed in the doorway as he went in. He'd be trapped in there.

Then Rich remembered the former barber's shop. But he could never get the door open and closed again in time. There was something else though – Chuck had joked about a cupboard under the stairs…

There was no obvious door, and Rich pressed his hands against the wooden panelling at the side of the staircase. The sound of the man descending the stairs got louder every second. The footsteps approaching along the corridor hesitated.

"That you, Kent?"

"You'd better hope so, Tom," the man on the stairs called back.

Rich pushed again at the panelling, harder this time.

And felt it give.

Just a little. Just enough for him to be sure – to *know* – why the woman was facing away, why she looked like she'd been running when she was shot. The woman had been running from the cupboard behind the door, which must have closed behind her. Then someone in the corridor had shot her from in front.

The footsteps started again. Rich scrabbled desperately at the panelling – pushing, prodding, probing, feeling for any way in.

A shadow fell across the bottom of the stairs. The man started to turn.

Suddenly Rich was falling through the panel. He had no idea how he'd managed it, but the relief that he was through the door – and that the opening panel made no sound as it opened or as he pushed it gently closed behind him – almost overwhelmed him.

The cupboard under the stairs was bigger than he had

imagined. There were several steps down, and the room continued under the stairway and round a corner, making an L-shaped room.

Rich just stood and stared. "Oh my God," he breathed.

The sound of gunfire had subsided. There were occasional isolated shots, but they were increasingly rare. Chuck led the way along narrow corridors and small offices as he took a convoluted back route to the Chief of Staff's office on the opposite side of the building from the Oval Office.

"Wouldn't the Situation Room be a better option?" Halford asked.

"Compromised," Chuck told him. "If there was anyone friendly down there, they'd have sorted this out by now. Or at least cleared the airwaves." He tapped his earpiece. "Still no signal. And the hostage takers have initiated a lock-down."

"What's that mean?" Jade whispered.

"It means we're trapped in here," the President told her. "Doors are all sealed. Windows are locked. The outer doors are all reinforced with armour plate, and all the glass is blast-proof." He gave a grim smile. "There's no place like home."

"Right," said Chuck, "we're almost there. Just got to

get across the main corridor, then we'll be safe. I know it goes against the grain, Mr President, but then we can sit this out and wait for rescue."

The President nodded. "Very well. But you're right – it sticks in the gut."

"There is another consideration, sir," Chuck added. "They have the Football. If they get you as well…"

"Then they get the authorisation for the launch codes. As you know, things are never quite as simple as they appear," said the President, "but I do take your point, Agent White."

Chuck signalled for them all to wait as he checked the corridor. He pointed to the door they were aiming for – on the other side of the corridor and a little way further along.

"Right – go!" he hissed, taking up position in the corridor, gun at the ready. Agent Harris was facing the other way along the corridor, also with his gun poised.

Jade reached the door first. She shoved it open and hurried inside. The sound of a gunshot made her turn in fear and surprise.

Agent Harris was falling to the floor, clutching his chest. Quick as lightning, Halford scooped up the agent's fallen gun and returned fire. Chuck grabbed the President and shoved him after Jade, before diving through the door.

"Come on, Halford!" Chuck yelled.

But Halford slammed the door shut behind them. "I'll hold them off," he yelled above the sound of more gunfire, muffled by the heavy door.

Then the gunfire stopped.

With the President's help, Chuck dragged a heavy desk across the room and rammed it up against the door. "We only need a minute," he said.

"But what about Dex?"

Chuck looked pale and drained. "We've lost a lot of good people today. Good friends. I'm sorry." He squeezed Jade's shoulder. Then abruptly he turned away. "Let's make sure it was worth the sacrifice. Mr President, I need your personal identity code."

"I think you probably know what it is anyway," said the President. He followed Chuck over to another door. There was a keypad beside it.

Chuck keyed in a number, and the door opened, revealing a small office the other side. The President keyed in his personal number, and another door opened. A hidden door, perfectly concealed in the wooden panelling of the wall.

"The Secure Area," Chuck told Jade. "It'll be cosy, but I think we'll manage."

There was a hammering sound from outside. Then a burst of gunfire. The heavy desk shifted back from the outer door by several centimetres.

Jade and the President didn't need any further encouragement. They hurried through the concealed door, and Chuck swung it shut behind them. It clicked back into place, and a light came on.

"I'm hoping they'll think we went through to the outer office," said Chuck. "There's no way they know about this place."

"We hope," the President added.

Jade said nothing. She was looking around the small room. It might have been a comfortable sitting room in a tiny city apartment. A bench-sofa ran round two of the walls. There was an upright chair in front of a desk, equipped with a telephone and a laptop computer. A photograph of the White House hung on one of the panelled wood walls.

Jade sat down on the sofa and slipped off her shoes. She rubbed her aching feet. "I'm never wearing heels again," she muttered.

Chuck immediately went to the telephone and lifted

the handset. "Dead as a doornail. Just like the comms and the cell phones."

"Blocked from the Situation Room?" the President asked.

"Or jammed from outside. I think we must assume, Mr President, that we are staying here for the duration. May I suggest you activate the Dog Whistle?"

The President nodded solemnly and adjusted his wrist watch.

Jade tried to push all thoughts of what might have happened to Rich and Dex out of her mind. "So, we just have to sit here? And what's a dog whistle? I mean, I know what a dog whistle is, but I'm guessing that's not what you're talking about. Right?"

Chuck nodded. "Right. The President's watch is fitted with an ultra-high frequency transmitter. It should be far enough up the scale to avoid being jammed. It's like a distress call, a mayday signal and locator so the special forces can find us. We call it the Dog Whistle."

"The problem with dog whistles," Jade told him, "is that it's not only dogs that can hear them."

14

They had moved the bodies out of the Situation Room and dumped them in the Secret Service offices.

"Close the door," Kent told Tom. "I don't want to have to look at that mess every time I go past."

"Sure thing."

Back in the Situation Room, Lorraine was at the main control desk. "You'd think they would have surveillance *inside* the White House," she said. The monitors were flashing up a succession of images – mostly of the outside of the house, but also CNN, Fox News, and other TV channels. Weather information appeared, then satellite pictures. A feed from a computer gave an error message that there was no input connected. None of the screens showed the corridors and rooms of the house's interior.

"Just a few of the main access areas."

"We got all the Secret Service agents?"

"I think so. It's gone quiet. There might be the odd loner, but we're properly armed now."

"And no sign of the President?" Kent asked.

"He's still inside, that's for sure. We got the place locked down tight before he was out of the Roosevelt Room."

"Then we'll find him." Kent hefted the Secret Service pistol he was carrying. "Guess we'll just have to do this the old-fashioned way. At least till help arrives."

"If it does," Tom muttered.

One of the monitors was showing a distant view of Pennsylvania Avenue. They could see tanks and army trucks parked on the street.

"Hey – they've been right so far. We'd never be here if it wasn't for them. They have some serious contacts."

"What if the army drive a tank into this place? Or start shooting missiles at us?" Tom asked.

"And risk killing the hostages, maybe even the President? They won't do that. We know they won't do that. So far as they are aware we have the President. Remember, there's a lot riding on this for a lot of people."

"Vested interests," said Lorraine. "Power plays.

Politics." She said it like it was a swear word.

"Whatever works," Kent told her. "You think I want to be here, doing this? Hell, I'd rather be raising my kids and holding down a proper job. But those Chinese will lock up good Americans without trial and steal the food out of our mouths as easy as they're taking our jobs and stifling our industry. Someone's got to make a stand."

"Yeah, right." Lorraine turned away. "The million dollars our friends from Wiengwei are paying each of us will help too, of course."

Kent grinned. "Of course. But then our goals and aspirations dovetail beautifully."

The top of the sofa lifted up. Inside was a large storage area filled with packets of dried food, bottled water, and various other supplies. Chuck opened a panel in the wall, and took out a box of ammunition. He reloaded his gun.

"Worried about your friend?" the President asked Jade quietly. "And your brother?"

Jade nodded. "I hate not knowing what's going on."

The President nodded. "I know. I'm just glad my wife and kids are out of town. But I've got some good friends out there, as has Agent White. It's difficult, but Chuck's right. We sit tight here and wait for help."

"If it comes," said Jade. "I just wish there was something we could do. We don't even know if this dog whistle thing is being heard. Maybe they think we're all dead."

Rich would do something, Jade thought. He'd have a plan. He'd work out some way of getting a message to the people outside – to Dad, even. But how?

"They'll know where we are," Chuck was telling her. "And they know the President is alive and well. The watch detects the President's pulse and transmits his vital signs as well as the mayday signal. They'll come for us."

Jade nodded. "I know." But she still felt helpless. What would Rich or Dad do, she wondered. She looked round the plain, almost empty room. What *could* they do?

The whole wall was covered with screens. There were a dozen of them, operated from a control desk. Rich sat in one of the two office chairs at the desk and stared in amazement at the pictures.

Each screen showed a different part of the White House. He guessed there was a way of controlling which camera's image was fed to each screen, but for the moment Rich just stared.

On one screen he could see the two men and the red-haired woman in the Situation Room. Another showed the carnage in the Secret Service offices. A third screen showed the stairway above him. Other screens showed rooms he didn't recognise. Maybe they were in the main house, or another wing... But he could see the Roosevelt Room – music stands overturned, buffet food scattered with broken crockery across the floor. The raiders seemed to have made this their base – Rich could see several people talking and waving guns...

And he watched Jade, Chuck White, and the President close the hidden door set into the wood panelling of the Chief of Staff's office. At least they were safe – for the moment, anyway.

At the side of the wall, one of the monitors gave a view of a large room with a sparkling chandelier hanging from the ceiling. The guests from the reception – including the two Chinese delegates – sat on the floor, hands on their heads. Rich could see three of the raiders, two men and a woman with close-cropped dark hair, standing in the room, pistols at the ready. Rich breathed another heartfelt sigh of relief as he saw a fourth gunman shove a groggy looking Dex Halford into the room to join the other hostages.

The control desk had a number pad set into it, and

Rich saw that each of the screens had a number printed on its frame. Beside the number pad was a joystick like a games console, and several buttons and knobs.

One of the men was leaving the Situation Room. He walked past the camera, going out of frame. The man didn't seem to see the camera, and Rich didn't recall noticing them in any of the rooms. They must be concealed. The woman who was lying dead outside had been monitoring events in the White House for the Secret Service.

She must have seen what was happening and run for help, Rich realised. Her cell phone and radio would have been jammed just like all the other communications.

Rich pressed 7 on the keypad – the number on the edge of the screen showing the Situation Room. Then he moved the joystick. As he had hoped, the camera moved in response, the image panning across as it followed the man who was leaving.

The man appeared on another monitor on the other side of the wall – the corridor. Rich keyed the joystick to this camera, and followed the man's journey. He went up the stairs, and Rich could hear the faint sound of his tread above him.

At the top of the stairs, the man continued towards the

Roosevelt Room. On another screen, the people in the room turned as the man came in. Rich could see their faces now. One of them was Kate Hunter.

There was a triangular volume graphic printed beside one of the knobs. Rich keyed the controls to the Roosevelt Room camera, and turned the knob.

"I'm glad someone has time to waste," a voice said. It came from right behind Rich – a rasping, husky whisper loaded with authority and disdain.

Rich whirled round in the chair. But there was no one there.

"In case you hadn't noticed, we appear to have mislaid the President of the United States of America." The voice came from a small speaker set high on the back wall. "So can I humbly suggest that you get out there…" The husky voice rose to an angry snarl, "… and find him!"

There were murmurs of apology, and people hurried from the room. Rich saw them emerge into the corridor, setting off in different directions as they hurried to search each of the rooms in the West Wing.

"Not you."

Kate Hunter stopped, and turned to face the man. She was as tall as he was. Her expression was unreadable on the grainy monitor.

"I'm still not sure about you," the man went on. "You seem so helpful, so willing, so amenable. But you know, I haven't seen those words converted into actions. I haven't witnessed your commitment."

"You want me to help, then give me a gun," Kate snapped back.

The man ignored her comment. He walked slowly around the room, not even looking at her as he spoke. "You know, when I told you all what the target really was, there was excitement. Exhilaration, even. From everyone – except you." Now the man did look at Kate. "Why *was* that?" he demanded.

She shrugged. "The White House – it's a big thing. More than gatecrashing some senator's party."

"But you weren't scared. I could tell that. You knew we could do it. Maybe it comes back to that commitment I mentioned."

"Maybe it comes back to being angry you didn't trust us with the truth."

"You're a clever lady. Did it not occur to you that holding a senator hostage was never going to get us very far? Oh, we could insist on the return of our airmen. And we could make our little demands for trade sanctions and official support for the freedom fighters in Wiengwei. But what would that really achieve?"

"What does *this* really achieve?"

"Once we have the President safe and sound, I'll show you."

"The President? What can he really do about your friends in Wiengwei?" Kate asked. "You'll just have the same petty demands for him too."

"Oh no." The man had stopped by the table where the buffet had been laid out. There was something on the table, and Rich moved the camera to see what it was.

A metal briefcase. Slumped in a chair beside it, Rich recognised Steve. He hoped the man was just unconscious.

"When we get the President," the man said, "we can use the launch codes. Our demands will be far from petty, I can tell you. And if the Chinese government refuses to recognise Marshal Wieng and the state of Wiengwei, then we'll wipe Beijing off the map."

Kate just stared. "You're kidding. They'll never believe your bluff."

But Rich could tell she knew as well as he did that the man wasn't kidding. He drummed his fingers on the top of the briefcase.

"It's no bluff," he rasped. "But maybe you're right.

Maybe they won't believe it. Maybe they won't believe we're really serious until the first missiles drop from the sky, and they start to count the dead."

15

General Wilson was not a happy man. John Chance could tell that at once. The first light of dawn was streaking the sky behind the White House, throwing tanks and armoured vehicles into silhouette. Soldiers stood like dark statues against the brightening horizon.

Many of the curtains were drawn in the West Wing of the White House, and the glass was specially treated so that directional microphones couldn't pick up sounds from inside. There was no vibration that could be turned back into sound waves.

The general shook his head, like he couldn't believe that his superiors at the Pentagon had really agreed that this annoying Brit and his even more annoying boss should be involved in events.

Chance smiled. He knew just how irritating Ardman could be, and he was glad that he wasn't on the receiving end of it for a change. He was also glad that Ardman had come in person. He was all too aware that whatever was happening inside the White House – and no one seemed to know what that was – Rich and Jade were right in the thick of it.

Ardman turned a slow circle, making a point of examining the assembled troops, tanks, trucks and other equipment that General Wilson had just been describing.

"Yes, it's all very impressive," Ardman said. "Troops, equipment, a complete – and very effective – media blackout. But tell me, what exactly do we know about what's going on? And what precisely have you done about it?"

"Not a lot we *can* do," Wilson said. "We've lost all contact with the staff and guests inside the West Wing. The whole place is locked down, which can only be done from inside. The Secret Service agents on duty at the doorway between the West Wing and the Mansion House reported gunfire as the blast shutters came down."

"So you don't even know if the President is alive?" said Chance.

"Oh, he's alive. At least, his heart's still beating."

Wilson turned and strode over to the enormous truck that was his mobile HQ. He didn't look to see if Ardman and Chance were following, but he carried on talking. "We call it the Dog Whistle. The President wears it at all times, and it relays his vital signs. Measures his sweat, his body temperature, his pulse."

The inside of the truck was a large operations room. Work stations down each side were manned by uniformed troops. There was a background buzz of noise from the equipment, from the soldiers updating each other as the situation developed, and from the radios and video-communications links.

Halfway down, General Wilson stopped at a screen. He pointed over the shoulder of the female soldier sitting at the work station in front of the main screen.

"That's his temperature. This trace is his heartbeat. If we can get close enough with this…" He picked up a small black box similar to a TV remote control but with a small screen set into it above the various buttons. "…then we can track the President to within centimetres. We can get a satellite fix too, of course. But that's only accurate enough to tell us which side of the building he's on."

"So, apart from knowing he's alive and well, we're none

the wiser," Ardman said. "I assume he *is* well?"

The woman turned from the screen. "His heart rate is slightly up. But I imagine he's in a stressful situation."

"I imagine he is," Ardman agreed.

The woman turned her attention back to the monitor. Almost at once a buzzer sounded insistently. The peaking line that was the President's heartbeat went flat – a single point of light running sideways across the monitor.

"We've lost him!" the woman exclaimed.

"Test the signal," Wilson ordered.

"Signal's fine, sir. There's no heartbeat. His temperature's dropping."

The light jumped. Then it was flat again.

"What's that?" General Wilson demanded. "Is he arresting?"

The woman shook her head. "Not a cardiac arrest. Not like that," she went on as the light jumped again. It traced a frenzy of peaks and troughs like an earthquake monitor.

"What the hell? It's all over the place."

The heartbeat stopped again. Then it bleeped in a steady rhythm. But not the rhythm of a normal human heart.

"What is that?" Ardman asked. "There's a pattern."

Chance was staring at the screen. "Can you get sound?

Like on a hospital machine?"

The woman glanced at Wilson, who nodded. She adjusted a control and the sound of the President's heart monitor came clearly from a speaker beside the screen. Three steady pulses, then another three longer bleeps, followed again by three shorter ones. The pattern repeated.

"I don't think that's the President's heart," said Chance. "Not unless he can make it beat in Morse code."

The President's watch lay open on the desk in the Secure Area. Chuck White was tapping carefully inside with the edge of the blade of his pocket knife. Every time he completed a connection between two tiny terminals, the watch's tiny transmitter sent a signal. The longer he held down the connection, the longer the signal. He hoped. He had no way of knowing for sure if it was actually working.

"Let's hope that got their attention," said Chuck. "You got the message yet, Mr President?"

"My Morse is a little rusty, but maybe they can make sense of this." The President put down a sheet of paper on the desk beside the watch. The message was written out in capitals, with the Morse code beneath each letter.

As Chuck set to work, the President smiled at Jade.

"Good idea, Miss Chance. You might just have saved our lives."

"Lucky we had someone here who could write Morse code," said Jade.

"A skill I learned long ago, in another life," said the President. "I used to fly jets off aircraft carriers, and they teach you Morse code in the navy. Or used to, anyway. Didn't think it would come in handy again."

"Let's just hope there's someone out there who can understand it," said Chuck.

Chance was leaning over the workstation scribbling down the dots and dashes as the heart monitor bleeped.

"There must be someone round here who understands Morse code," said General Wilson. He marched off along the headquarters truck.

"It obviously hasn't occurred to him that us useless Brits might know how to read it," said Chance.

"Clearly not," Ardman agreed. "You know he's a member of the same golf club as the Vice President?"

"Is that important?" Chance was working his way through the Morse code message, writing the translation beneath each set of dots and dashes.

"Probably not. But it's interesting that the Vice

President chose last night to make a speech about how the Chinese should recognise the independence of Tibet and Wiengwei, and to demand they release those airmen they claim they don't have. He's rather less liberal than the President. Quite a hard liner in fact. And of course he'd take over if anything were to happen to the President…"

"Good job General Wilson's in charge then," said Chance quietly. He handed Ardman the decoded message.

White House Sealed. Estimate 12 raiders now with Secret Service handguns. Communications jammed. POTUS.

"Looks like he's all right for the moment," said Ardman as he read the last word on the paper. The signature: POTUS – President Of The United States. "Let's try and keep it that way."

General Wilson briefed the assault team in person. He had told Ardman and Chance in no uncertain terms that they were not to become involved in 'operational matters'. So while Ardman made a point of complaining, Chance slipped away and sat in the front of the assault team's plain black truck, listening through the partition.

He had heard more assault briefings than he could remember – and given a fair few as well.

"Obviously we want the hostages out safe and sound," Wilson was saying as he summed up. "But your number one priority is the President. You have a portable tracker that will lead you to the Dog Whistle, and it sounds like the President is wearing it again after signalling to us. We're as positive as we can be that the heartbeat is his. Oh, and before I hand you over to Captain Roberts, two operatives from G Division will be joining you for the breach. They'll keep out of the way, but act as backup."

Chance frowned. It was unusual – not to say dangerous – to add in people from another group to a team that had trained and operated together.

Sure enough, Captain Roberts was making the same point in the back of the operations truck.

"You have your orders, Captain," the General snapped. "I want belts and braces on this one. No foul-ups. G Division is there in case they're needed. Otherwise they'll keep well out of the way. Got it?"

"Sir."

"Very well. Brief your men. You've been over the plans and drawings. You've drawn up several possible scenarios. I want you ready to affect a breach in half an hour."

Chance waited until the General had gone before he climbed quietly out of the truck's cab. He waited with

Ardman a short way back from where the assault team was preparing. The members of the team gathered in the shadows, talking quietly to each other, going over their plan again and again, checking and double-checking plans and blueprints…

Half an hour passed quickly, despite the tension and anticipation.

Just as Captain Roberts was giving final instructions to his team, two more figures in black combat uniforms, heads covered by dark balaclavas, pushed past Chance and Ardman and hurried to join the assault team.

One of the figures was a man – stocky and powerfully built. The other was a woman, slim and athletic and tall – a contrast to her companion. She glanced at Chance as she pushed past him. For a moment his eyes met hers – visible for a second through the narrow slit in her black mask. Then she was gone.

Chance wished he was going with her – with the assault team. It went against the grain, but there was nothing he could do now except hope and pray Captain Roberts knew his stuff. He was impressed by the man's reputation, but a lot of it would come down to luck as well as meticulous planning. Of course, the team's priority would be the safety of the President, but Chance's children and his best friend were in there somewhere and he felt powerless to help them.

It wasn't a feeling he was used to, or that he liked, which was maybe why it took him a while to realise what he had just seen.

The team was moving into position. Quiet, calm, efficient orders were relayed over a radio link to the mobile HQ. Ardman and Chance listened in as they followed Wilson inside the truck.

Chance hesitated, one foot inside the operations room, the other on the step outside.

"What is it?" Ardman said, sensing the sudden change in Chance.

"Those two from G Division that General Wilson sent to join the team… The woman."

"What about her?"

Chance frowned. What indeed – there was something, something that made him suddenly uneasy and cold inside. He could see her again in his mind's eye – the quick glance at him, maybe a flash of recognition, then she was gone. Mind's *eye*…

"Her eyes," said Chance. "Tell Wilson to stop the breach. Her eyes were different colours."

And then he was running.

16

The sound of the explosion was magnified by the quiet of the early morning. A window in the Vice President's office was blown violently inwards.

Ideally, Captain Roberts would have liked to enter silently and retain the element of surprise. But that wasn't possible. This was the closest point to where they believed the President might be, based on the signal from the Dog Whistle.

Even so, Roberts' plan depended on the raiders inside the White House not knowing if, or when, or where his team would breach their defences.

Before the sound of the explosion had died away, he could hear shouting in his ear – the urgent voice of the mobile HQ.

"A-Force – break off. I repeat, break off. Do not breach at this time!"

"Too late," Roberts muttered into his throat microphone. There was no way they could stop now – who knew what damage would be done, how the raiders would respond. And they wouldn't get another chance to surprise the enemy after this.

He took the decision. "This is A-Force. We have already breached. We're going in."

He gestured for the team to continue. The first of the assault squad dived through the shattered windows. They rolled, came upright with their Heckler and Koch 9mm machine pistols levelled. More soldiers followed, moving ahead under cover from their colleagues. There were shouts and cries from deep inside the White House.

The team moved forwards with professional ease and deadly efficiency. One soldier kicked a door open, another lobbed a smoke grenade into the corridor outside.

Last to enter the Vice President's office were the two new members of the team from G Division.

In the Roosevelt Room, Kent looked up at the sound of the explosion.

"We've got company," said Kate Hunter.

Kent smiled. "About time too. I've been expecting them."

"Friends?" she asked sarcastically.

But Kent nodded. "Yes, actually. Let's go and greet them."

"Too late, sir," the communications officer said. "They've already breached."

General Wilson did not reply. Like Ardman beside him, he was listening to the sounds coming over the radios of the assault team.

They could hear the breathing of the men; their shouts to each other; the crump of a smoke grenade detonating; gunfire.

Wilson spoke to Ardman without looking at him. "Where's your man Chance?"

"Doing his job."

Chance was running across the White House lawn. He didn't bother trying to stay out of the floodlights and in the shadows as Captain Roberts' team had done. Speed, not stealth, was the important thing.

He saw the orange and black of the explosion, felt the thump of the shockwave in his chest, even though most of the blast was directed into the window frame. Ahead of him, dark figures were diving through the smoking windows. The last figure seemed to glance back before entering the White House.

From inside, Chance heard the sound of another, smaller explosion. Then automatic gunfire.

Cursing the fact he was unarmed, Chance hurled himself through the window. "Roberts!" he yelled.

But his voice was lost in the sound of another burst of gunfire. There were two figures ahead of him – standing in the doorway of the room. One was stocky and built like a bull, the other slender and tall. G-division. As the woman turned, the end of her long plaited hair whipped round.

Chance dived for cover as she fired at him. Bullets stitched a trail across the carpet. He rolled, leaped to his feet, and charged at the woman. She was still firing at where he had been a split second earlier. Chance's shoulder caught her gun and knocked it off target as she fired again. Plaster fell from the ceiling. One of the windows still intact after the blast crazed in a spider-web from the point of impact, but did not break.

The woman was knocked backwards, colliding with the stocky man as he turned.

"Out!" Chance yelled into the corridor. "A-Force – get out now!"

The corridor was full of smoke. There were dark shapes lying across it. One of them moved, crawling towards Chance. He ran to help. Another dark figure solidified out of the smoke. A shot from a handgun smacked into the wall close by as dark figures appeared through the gloom at the end of the corridor – the raiders.

Chance and another soldier grabbed the wounded man under the arms and dragged him back into the Vice President's office. The soldier loosed off a burst of gunfire – angry red flashes in the grey air that provoked more shots in return.

Several more soldiers were retreating. There was noise and confusion. But the firing from the raiders inside the White House seemed to have stopped.

"Where's Cyrus?"

"He's down. Art too."

"Hell! Let's get out of here."

"You'll be all right, sir," the soldier with Chance said to the man they had dragged back to the window.

Chance realised the wounded man was Captain Roberts. He was bleeding from just above the knee. All that was visible of his face was the area round his eyes, and his skin looked deathly pale against the black of his mask.

Another of the assault team took the Captain's arm, allowing Chance to run back and help yell for the rest of them to follow.

But there was no one else.

Eight men had gone into the White House, led by Roberts. Three were coming out again – three and John Chance.

But Chance knew there were two more somewhere in the smoky corridor. Two people who were not part of Roberts' team but had somehow infiltrated the military cordon round the White House. A man and a woman who had turned on the men who thought they were all on the same side.

He saw the distinctive silhouette of the woman in the grey ahead of him, and instinctively reached for his gun. A gun he didn't have.

The air erupted again with gunfire, and Chance sprinted back to the office, and dived out of the window after Roberts and the two other survivors of A-Force.

The noise of the explosion came from the speakers as well as from the floor above. It woke Rich, who had drifted off into a restless sleep, slumped over the control desk. He had no idea what time it was, but the monitors showed it was getting light outside.

He watched the assault team. The smoke and gunfire. The dark shapes of two of the team who seemed to be firing on their colleagues.

And then another figure – one that Rich recognised – arrived on the scene and changed the course of the fight.

Dad.

Rich almost ran from the room, but he had no idea of the geography. Where was this action taking place?

He could see the raiders, led by the man who had almost caught him on the stairs – Kent. There was no way Rich could get to Dad and escape through the shattered window.

He leaned back in the chair and watched as the smoke slowly cleared and the two black-clad raiders pulled off their masks.

They were oriental, and Rich recognised them both. One of them was a man with close-cropped black hair. He was stocky, but even on the screen Rich got the impression his bulk was muscle rather than fat. His face was round, almost like a baby's.

The woman with him shook out a long plait of jet back hair. Together with the man she collected up the automatic weapons from the fallen assault team.

Even though he'd seen her only briefly at the hospital in England, Rich knew at once who it was. It was Colonel Shu, and Rich recognised the man with her from the TV news reports.

Marshal Wieng.

Rich turned up the volume as Kent and several of the raiders arrived. Kent and the Marshal stared at each other for several moments. Then Wieng gave a loud burst of laughter and embraced the other man, slapping him heartily on the back.

"I'm glad you and the colonel could join us, sir," said Kent as they separated. "Our mutual friend made sure your new passports wouldn't arouse interest at the airports."

"All very efficient," Wieng said, his English only lightly accented. "And how efficiently are things proceeding here?"

"The White House is secured. I see you've brought us some decent weapons. Thank you. Shame about the hole in the window, but I'll leave two men on guard here in case they try to come back in this way."

"And the President?" Wieng asked.

Kent turned away. "I'm afraid we don't have him yet,"

he said in his hoarse, whispering voice. "But he's somewhere inside the sealed area of the White House. We'll track him down soon."

Colonel Shu picked something up from beside one of the fallen soldiers. Rich couldn't see it clearly, but it looked like a black box, about the size and shape of a television remote control. She handed it to Marshal Wieng.

The Marshal hefted the box in his hand. "I think we can track down the President more easily than you imagine," he said.

17

"A locator?" Kent rasped.

"The President is fitted with a tracking device," Colonel Shu explained. "It never leaves him, and this tracker will lead us to it."

"The American Special Forces intended to use it to find the President and rescue him." Marshal Wieng smiled. "The device will work just as well for us. Only we do not intend to rescue the President."

"Hell no," Kent agreed. "We need him here."

"Then let's go get him," said Colonel Shu.

Rich watched the conversation about the tracker in horrified fascination, every word amplified by the speakers in the secret observation room. He had seen the

President, Chuck White and Jade hiding behind a panel in one of the offices. He'd thought they were going to be safe, but now it looked as though they would be found at any moment.

He didn't even know where the office was. And if he did, he doubted he could get there before Kent and Marshal Wieng. But he knew he had to try. He might be safe here in the secret control room, but Rich was doing no one any good. He checked his mobile, and the sophisticated cell phone he'd taken from Steve. Neither of them had a signal.

It seemed unlikely that the phones in the Secret Service offices were working – they'd be easier to cut off than the cell phones. So the only place there might be a line out would be the Situation Room. On the screen he could see the red-haired woman and one of the gunmen working at a computer in there. Another dead end – they'd take him captive as soon as they saw him. If they didn't shoot him first.

Knowing that Dad was out there somewhere spurred Rich on. No way was he going to sit back and watch while Jade was in trouble and Dad was working to rescue them. Rich turned the sound right down on the monitor, and listened at the door for any noise from outside.

Gently, he eased the door open. There was no sign of anyone in the corridor. Just the faint sound of voices from the Situation Room. Rich tip-toed around the end of the stairs and started up them, as quickly and quietly as he could.

At the top he paused again, listening. There was shouting from somewhere in the distance, but it didn't seem that there was anyone nearby.

So far as he could tell, this floor of the White House was a large square. There were several function rooms in the middle – including the Roosevelt Room where the reception had been – and the corridor ran round them, with offices and conference rooms on the outside edge.

Rich didn't recognise the office where Jade was concealed as being one he had seen before, so he set off to the right – along the section of corridor he'd not been down before. At any moment Marshal Wieng or Kent or one of the gunmen might appear as they hunted down the President, so Rich kept close to the wall, ready to dart into a room or an alcove as soon as he heard anyone coming.

He checked every room as he passed, but the problem was, a lot of them were offices. And one office looks very much like another in the same building. He tried to think if there were any particular features of the room where

Jade and the others had hidden. A desk – great. And a large photograph of the White House on the wall. Not helpful – lots of the offices had a picture of the White House. Most of them had similar wooden panelling. None of it responded or opened when he tried to find a hidden door at the point he recalled.

A desk… Of course, they'd dragged the desk over to block the door. He needed to find an office where the desk had been moved…

At the corner of the corridor, Rich paused again. Now he could hear something – voices, and running feet. Were they coming his way? He risked a look round the corner, and saw Kent and Marshal Wieng, followed by Colonel Shu and two other gunmen. They were hurrying towards him, and Rich ducked back out of sight.

But before he could run for cover, the sound of their footsteps stopped.

"In here!" Colonel Shu announced in a loud voice.

"Gotcha," Kent's amplified whisper was full of anticipation.

Was he too late? Rich risked another look. He saw the last of the gunmen hurrying inside one of the rooms further along the corridor.

"Oh, Jade," Rich sighed. It looked like he was too late.

He edged along the corridor, desperate to hear what was happening even though he knew he was risking his freedom – maybe his life.

There was a large framed picture on the wall opposite the room where Wieng and the others had gone. It looked like an aerial photograph of the White House, but the light was reflecting off the glass covering the picture. Rich edged slightly closer, and the reflection became clearer. He could see the vague images of the men inside the room.

"Here. Behind this wall."

Rich was close enough to hear Marshal Wieng's excited exclamation.

"But there's no way in," someone else said – one of the other gunmen.

"It's a safe area," said Kent. "A panic room. It'll be locked solid."

In the reflection, Rich saw the men in the room draw back. One of them raised a gun.

The sound of machine-gun fire echoed from the room.

"See, behind the wood. Metal. A sealed box," Kent was saying.

"The bullets have barely marked it," said Colonel Shu.

"Get this wooden panelling off," Kent growled. "There must be a way to get inside."

"We'll blow our way in if we have to," Marshal Wieng decided. "We have him now!"

There was nothing Rich could do here now, he realised. He made his way back carefully towards the stairs, desperately trying to think of some way he could help. Maybe he could cause a diversion – but that would only postpone the inevitable. Marshal Wieng and Kent knew where the President was now. Rich might slow them down, distract them, but they would soon return to the job of breaking into the panic room. Jade and the others were trapped, and there was nothing Rich could do to rescue them.

But, he thought, they weren't the only people in danger here. If Wieng and Kent were concentrating on capturing the President, then perhaps – just perhaps – Rich could help someone else…

Head down, deep in thought, wondering where the hostages were being kept, Rich was soon back at the stairs. He was so engrossed that he didn't hear the sound of footsteps until it was too late.

Someone was coming up the stairs. And Rich had nowhere to hide.

He pressed back against the wall. The dark shape of a man appeared at the top of the stairs. A man holding a handgun. If he just continued straight on along the corridor, he wouldn't see Rich. But if he turned to go along the corridor in the same direction as Rich had been…

The man turned.

His eyes widened in surprise as he saw Rich standing by the wall.

"Oh, er – hi," said Rich.

The man's mouth twisted into a smile and he raised the gun.

The sound of the gunfire was muffled inside the secure area. Jade could just make out the shouts of the people outside.

"I think they've found us," said the President.

"Can they get in?" Jade wondered.

"This place is designed to survive a direct hit from a bunker-buster bomb," Chuck assured her. "There's no way they can get in."

"Unless they pick the lock," Jade told him.

"Not that easy. It's electronic. It has a five-digit code, and after three wrong attempts it resets and locks them out."

"I bet it resets as 1 2 3 4 5 then," said Jade.

"How the hell did you know that?" said Chuck. "Just kidding," he added as he saw Jade's expression.

"Thanks," said Jade. "You nearly saw what I had for lunch then."

"You got me too," said the President. "And I know what the code is. So you're sure we're safe in here."

"We are, Mr President. We just sit tight."

"But what about the others – out there?" Jade asked. "How safe are they?"

"Once these people realise they can't get in by brute force," said Chuck, "then not very. Mr President," he said grimly, "sooner or later I'm afraid you're going to have to make a decision. Whatever you decide, you have my full support."

Jade felt suddenly cold. "What decision?"

"Whether I give myself up," said the President, "or pay the price for my staying safe in here. And Agent White is correct. That price is likely to be in blood."

"You mean, if we don't give ourselves up, they'll start to kill the hostages?"

The President nodded. "I'm afraid that's exactly what I mean."

18

Without thinking, Rich launched himself at the man. He felt his shoulder slam into the man's stomach and heard him gasp with surprise as the wind was knocked from him. Rich crashed into the wall at the top of the stairs, as the man fell back. Off balance, he threw his arms out to try to save himself. Rich grabbed for the gun – and missed. The man was falling backwards, and Rich could only watch as he tumbled down the stairs.

The gun dropped, clattering after the falling man. His hand scrabbled for the banister rail. He turned a full circle, crashing down head first on to his back. The man then slid and rolled to the bottom of the staircase. His outstretched hand flopped down close to the gun.

Rich prepared to run. He expected the man to recover

the gun and fire, but he didn't move. Was it a trick? Warily, Rich descended a couple of steps. He was ready to run at the first sign of movement.

But the man still didn't move. Rich looked around. Had anyone heard? How much noise had they made? Did his attacker cry out? Rich couldn't remember. All he could hear was the blood thumping in his ears as he hurried down the rest of the stairs.

There was a trail of blood down the last few steps. The man's eyes were wide open, staring up at Rich but seeing nothing. The back of his head was a tangled mess of red. Rich looked away, feeling suddenly sick.

Fighting back his nausea, Rich scooped up the gun while trying not to look at the man's body. He pushed the gun into the pocket of his suit. He couldn't afford for anyone to find the body, he realised. If they did, they'd know someone was still free and hunt him down. They might ignore the blood – there was enough of that around the place already.

Listening for any sign of someone coming, Rich put his hands under the man's arms. Struggling to keep his stomach in check he dragged the man into the Secret Service offices. He was heavy, and Rich was exhausted by the time he got him inside. He dumped the body behind a desk and hoped no one would look there.

His hands were stained red, and Rich wiped them as best he could on his handkerchief.

"Dragging dead bodies round the White House," he murmured to himself. "Not something I want to make a habit of."

The guests from the reception and a couple of surviving Secret Service agents, together with the White House staff – secretaries, cleaners, the press liaison team – and the two Chinese dignitaries were gathered in the largest of several function rooms.

Dark portraits of former presidents looked down from the walls. Ornate chandeliers cast glittering light across the room. All the furniture had been pushed to the walls so the centre of the room was clear.

The prisoners sat on the floor as four of their captors stood guard over them. There were three men and a woman, grim-faced, pacing back and forth. One of the men now had a Heckler and Koch 9mm machine pistol salvaged from the ill-fated assault team.

Halford struggled to get comfortable on the floor. It was difficult with a false leg. He'd been caught in a fire-fight in Afghanistan and lost his leg below the knee years ago – it was John Chance who had carried him to safety.

"Keep still," the woman told him, jabbing her handgun in Halford's direction to make the point. She had close-cropped dark hair so it looked like her head had been stained. Halford had heard one of the other gunmen call her Marcie.

Halford didn't reply. From the sounds of the explosion and gunfire he could guess what had happened – an unsuccessful attack by the US Special Forces. The gunmen would now be elated they had won that encounter, but also anxious and nervous about the future. A lethal mixture.

Without a gun, Halford had known he didn't have a hope against the attackers who were after the President. He had expected to be shot down and killed, but instead of a bullet the gun had fired a tranquiliser dart that caught him in the arm. He pulled it out at once, but immediately felt groggy. The gunmen had been amused rather than annoyed, content to knock him to the floor and kick him savagely before dragging him to join the other hostages.

The leader – Kent – had soon satisfied himself that Halford really didn't know where the Secret Service agents were taking the President, and had lost interest in him. Now Halford was keeping his head down, trying to blend in with the other hostages and not draw attention to himself. Luckily for him, the gunmen seemed to be keeping a closer eye on the two Chinese. Halford's leg was a problem, though. He tried to relax and ignore the discomfort of sitting awkwardly on the floor, and the residual headache from the drug in the dart. Sooner or later he would get an opportunity to escape or overpower his captors, and he was determined to take it.

The opportunity arrived in the shape of Rich. He was standing outside the open door of the room, out of sight of the gunmen. It wasn't just Halford who could see him, though. A woman gave a barely stifled gasp. People turned to see what others were looking at. In a moment, one of the gunmen would look too.

Halford struggled to his feet. It wasn't easy with his false leg. "We've been here all night," he announced. "And I need the bathroom."

There was immediate support and agreement from the other hostages.

In the noise and confusion, Rich had ducked out of sight. Halford hoped he had heard what was happening.

"All right, all right," the woman called Marcie shouted above the noise. The noise continued, and she fired a shot into the ceiling. Plaster fell in a shower. There was silence.

"We'll organise you in groups of three. Any trouble, you get shot – is that clear?"

There were murmurs of assent.

"I asked first," said Halford. It was a gamble; they might make him wait till last for causing trouble. But he hoped they'd assume he was getting desperate.

"You and two others." The woman picked two men close to Halford who'd immediately put their hands up. She turned to the gunman with the machine pistol. "Leon – you take them."

"I'm a nursemaid now," Leon complained. He sighed. "Right, come on then. And like she said – don't try anything funny."

There was a gents restroom diagonally opposite across the corridor. Leon ushered the three men inside. There were several urinals, and a cubicle. Halford made immediately for the cubicle. He pushed the door closed behind him.

"Hey!" Leon shouted.

"Only be a minute," Halford called back. "Or do you want to watch?"

Rich grinned at the comment. He was sitting on the lowered lid of the toilet, his feet drawn up so they couldn't be seen under the door. Halford smiled back, and put his finger to his lips. Rich had a pad of paper and a pen he'd borrowed from one of the offices. He showed Halford the first sheet on the pad:

President, Jade and Chuck are sealed in a panic room. But the bad guys know where they are and are trying to get in.

Dad's outside somewhere – bad guys drove back the special forces. Marshal Wieng and Colonel Shu are in charge!

What's going on?!

Halford gave an exaggerated shrug at the last question. He took the pad and pen and scribbled quickly:

They want the President. Must be to do with the Wiengwei rebels' cause.

Guess we have to sit tight till help arrives. Don't do anything stupid.

Rich nodded, and took the pad back.

As if.

I got you a present.

Halford frowned. "A present?" he mouthed.

"Hey you, British guy! Hurry up in there," Leon shouted from outside. There was a sudden hammering on the cubicle door. "If you're not out in thirty seconds, I'm coming in to get you."

"Just coming," Halford called back.

Rich took something from his jacket pocket and gave it to Halford. A handgun.

Halford stared at it. He could take out Leon, get the man's gun… But someone would hear the shots. Marcie and her friends were only metres away across the corridor. He wouldn't last long. So he nodded and smiled and pushed the gun into his waistband at the small of his back.

"See you," Halford mouthed. He flushed the toilet, then opened the door just enough to slip out without Leon being able to see inside.

"About time."

The other two men were waiting beside Leon. The Secret Service agent raised his eyebrows at Halford, maybe guessing that he was up to something. Halford kept his expression neutral and walked quickly towards the door.

"Hey!" Leon called after him. "Just a minute."

Halford stopped. He braced himself, ready to reach for the gun. He turned slowly and carefully, to find Leon walking towards him, gun raised, a look of contempt on his face.

"In this country," Leon said, "we wash our hands afterwards."

Halford muttered an apology, and complied.

Rich waited until he heard the door close behind Halford and the others before he came out of the cubicle. He stuffed the notebook and pen into his jacket pocket. It didn't quite fit. He wasn't sure if Halford would get a chance to use the gun, but Rich was sure the ex-SAS soldier was more qualified to look after it than he was.

He slipped quietly out of the restroom. The woman with very short dark hair was organising another group of hostages. Rich needed to be quick to get out of sight before the gunman came back with them. He ran on tiptoe to the nearest corner of the corridor.

Straight into the two men coming the other way. It was Kent and Marshal Wieng.

Rich skidded to a halt, turned and started to run back the way he'd come. But the gunman with the next group of hostages was standing in font of him.

Rich stopped. There was nowhere else to go. He put his hands up and closed his eyes, silently cursing his bad luck.

Marshal Wieng looked from Rich to the restroom door and back again. "He was in there." He reached out and grabbed Rich's face, holding his jaw tight as he forced Rich to look at him. "What were you doing in there?" he demanded.

"It's the restroom," Rich gasped painfully. Wieng's fingers were digging into his cheeks. "What do you think I was doing?"

With his other hand, Wieng pulled the notepad from Rich's pocket. "Taking notes?" he mused, opening the cover to examine the first page.

It was blank. Rich felt a wave of relief that he'd torn out the pages he and Halford had written on and stuffed them deep into the waste bin full of paper towels in the restroom when he came out of the cubicle.

Marshal Wieng let go of Rich. "Just a boy," he said. "I should have you shot for eluding us. But who wants to see a boy die?" He turned away.

But Kent was watching Rich with sudden interest. "You're right, Marshal Wieng. No one wants to see a kid get shot. Not you, not me. And sure as hell not the President of the United States of America."

Marshal Wieng nodded. "A good idea."

Kent raised his machine pistol and jabbed it hard into Rich's ribs. "I've got a little job for you to do, son. I've a feeling you might be the key we've been looking for."

After the disastrous Special Forces operation, General Wilson had convened a meeting with his top advisors. Ardman and

Chance were not invited. Wilson had already made it clear that he didn't believe Chance's account of events and that he must have misinterpreted what he saw in the heat of battle. He refused to accept that the two black-clad special operatives had turned out to be Colonel Shu and Marshal Wieng – though he did at least grudgingly thank Chance for getting Captain Roberts out of the White House.

The Vice President had been flown in by helicopter, and Ardman made a point of pushing through the ranks of troops and bodyguards to greet him like an old friend. The Vice President seemed confused, but shook Ardman's hand before joining General Wilson in the mobile headquarters truck.

"I didn't know you were friends with the Vice President," Chance told Ardman as they sat in the back of an army truck drinking strong coffee.

"Never met him before," Ardman confessed. "Just thought I ought to be friendly."

That didn't sound very plausible, but Chance let it go. "I wonder what he and General Wilson are talking about, closeted away in the headquarters vehicle."

Ardman put down his coffee on the floor between his feet, and took two small earpieces from his pocket. He gave one to Chance. "Let's find out, shall we?"

Chance shook his head in disbelief. "You put a bug on the Vice President?"

"It must have fallen into his pocket when I shook his hand."

The voice of the Vice President was loud and clear in Chance's ear:

"...incredible. You're sure about this?"

"We've had positive identification, Mr Vice President. There can be no doubt," Wilson replied.

"But, on US soil? That's... unacceptable."

"Chinese Special Forces operate all over the world. We know the leaders in Beijing don't give a damn about anyone else's sovereignty. Look at how they've denied knowing anything about our airmen."

Chance turned to Ardman. "Wilson's claiming these guys are Chinese Special Forces? That's crazy. I saw Colonel Shu, and she's with the Wiengwei rebels."

Ardman held his hand up. General Wilson was speaking again.

"I'm afraid there can be no doubt, Mr Vice President. It's been confirmed at the highest levels at the Pentagon. And we know from the information we have from the British MI6 that the Chinese are after the Football. The nuclear launch codes."

"But why?"

"Isn't it obvious, sir? So they can launch our own missiles against us, and we'll have no way of defending ourselves."

"But that's unbelievable."

"Hear hear," Chance muttered.

"And the Pentagon have confirmed nothing of the sort," Ardman added.

"Our only option, sir," General Wilson was saying, "is to strike first."

There was silence for several moments. When the Vice President spoke, it was in a hushed whisper. "You mean…?"

"Yes, sir. We need your authorisation key to bypass the President's own personal nuclear codes, and launch a pre-emptive attack against mainland China. You have to authorise a first strike."

There had been silence for several minutes. Jade was beginning to think that the attackers had given up and decided just to leave them inside the secure room.

But then it started again. Only this time it was different. Instead of an angry hammering of metal on metal, there was a polite knock. Like they wanted to be let in.

"Can you hear me in there?" The voice was muffled but clear, slightly accented. "I hope you can, because I've brought a friend to visit. Tell them your name, young man."

There was silence. Then, louder and angry: "I said tell them your name!"

Jade shuddered as there was a cry of pain. *Please let it not be—*

"My name is Rich." His voice trembled.

Jade's legs went weak. "They've got my brother," she said.

"You have ten seconds to open this door, Mr President," said the man's voice. "Unless you want the blood of this poor child on your hands. The clock is ticking. *One... Two...*"

"Decision time," said the President.

"*Three... Four...*"

"You cannot open that door, sir," said Chuck, ashen-faced.

"*Five... Six...*"

"No matter who it is they've got out there, you cannot open the door."

"*Seven... Eight...*"

The President nodded. He looked at Jade, his face

drained of all colour and expression. "I know what I have to do. And I'm sorry."

"*Nine…*"

Jade closed her eyes and turned away.

"*Ten.*"

19

"Wait!" the President shouted. "We're coming out."

Jade opened her eyes, almost sobbing with relief.

"Mr President," said Chuck White quietly.

"I know, Chuck – but what can I do?"

"It's all right, Mr President. For what it's worth, you've made the right moral choice."

"It's the only choice."

"Thank you," said Jade, her voice shaking.

"You're welcome," said the President. "Now, I need you to do something for me."

"We're waiting!" the voice shouted from outside.

"Just typing in the access codes," Chuck shouted back. "It'll take a few seconds."

The President put his hands on Jade's shoulders and

looked into her eyes. "We don't have much time."

Rich was on his knees. Kent had his machine pistol pressed against his temple, and Marshal Wieng was standing off to the side. For a few moments Rich had really thought he was going to die. It had surprised him how calm he stayed – the inevitability, the fact he could do nothing about it, made the whole situation seem unreal somehow.

Now that the President had said he was giving himself up, Rich was more frightened. What if he changed his mind? What if Kent shot him anyway? What would they do to Jade?

The wooden panelling had been ripped away from the metal door concealed beneath it. The door itself was scratched and scorched, dented by gunshots and blistered by explosions. After what seemed an age, the door clicked open, then swung heavily aside.

Chuck White was standing in the doorway, his hands raised in surrender. In one hand he held his pistol, which Marshal Wieng immediately took from him. Then Wieng grabbed Chuck's arm and heaved him out of the secure room. He reached past Chuck and grabbed the President by his suit lapels, pulling him out too.

The President staggered after Chuck. Kent had moved his gun from Rich's head, and tracked the President and Chuck with it. Wieng was looking round the concealed room. Satisfied, he stepped out into the office.

Rich frowned in confusion. "Where's…?"

Chuck glared at him, giving the tiniest shake of the head.

"What are you going to do with us?" Rich asked quickly, covering his first thought.

"Oh, I'm sure we'll think of something," Kent rasped.

But Rich barely heard him. He was staring through the open doorway into the small room beyond. Where was Jade?

Then Wieng pushed the door shut again. Kent stepped over to the numeric keypad set into the frame of the door. He slammed the butt of his gun down on it, shearing the pad from the wall in a shower of sparks.

"It's time we had a little talk, Mr President," said Kent. "Marshal Wieng needs your help. And one way or another, he's going to get it."

It was difficult to hear what was going on. But as soon as it was quiet, Jade gently pushed up the top cushions of the sofa. Lying inside the cupboard built into the bench seat was uncomfortable and cramped. There was only just room for her, even with some of the tins and cartons removed and stacked by the desk.

There was no way Chuck could have fitted inside. And the gunmen would expect the President to be with a Secret Service agent rather than a teenager.

The room was empty. The gunmen had gone. She'd heard the name of Marshal Wieng mentioned – was he really involved somehow? Was Colonel Shu here too?

Jade pushed aside the cushioned lid, and heaved herself out. She crept to the door and listened. Silence. With a sudden rush of relief, Jade pressed the button that she knew opened the door. She'd watched Chuck press it, seen the door click open, just as she lowered the top down on the sofa and hid.

Nothing happened. Maybe she hadn't pressed quite hard enough. Jade pressed the button again. Still nothing. She thumped the button, kicked the door, then swore at both.

But the door remained locked shut. It was like the mechanism from the button to the door controls was no longer connected.

She was trapped inside an impregnable room. No one could get in, but she had no way out either…

*

There was a soldier on guard outside the door into the mobile headquarters. He stepped in front of Ardman and Chance as they approached.

"General Wilson is in conference, gentlemen. If I can ask you to wait."

"You can ask," Ardman told him. He walked past the soldier reaching for the door.

The soldier turned, reaching for his handgun. But it was twisted from his grasp before he could level it.

"You've asked," Chance told him. "Don't push your luck any further than that." He slapped the gun back into the soldier's surprised hand. "Believe me, whether he wants to or not, General Wilson needs to see us."

He followed Ardman into the back of the enormous container lorry. At the far end was a small conference area where General Wilson was talking quietly with the Vice President.

Ardman strode past the soldiers manning the equipment. "General Wilson, Mr Vice President," he announced loudly and coldly. "I know what you're planning, and it stops right now."

Wilson was on his feet. "You don't know a thing. And I gave orders no one was to enter this headquarters for the time being."

"You mean until you'd arranged a nuclear strike against an innocent country?" Ardman shouted back down the length of the truck.

There was sudden silence as all activity stopped. The Vice President stood up, looking pale.

"We are discussing a variety of options," he snapped. "Who is this man?"

"British Intelligence," Wilson told him. "Yeah, there really is such a thing."

"Maybe it's time for you to exercise *your* intelligence, Mr Vice President," Ardman snapped back. "Are you really going to authorise a nuclear attack on the basis of General Wilson's say-so? On hearsay and rumour?"

Wilson was seething. He jabbed his finger at Ardman as they drew closer, facing each other in a stand-off. "Those raiders are working for the Chinese. They imprisoned our airmen without a trial and are now planning to launch our own missiles against us."

"And you know that how? What could they possibly gain? What evidence do you actually have for any of this? I tell you they are rebels from Wiengwei, not Chinese special forces at all. And for your information, we don't even know if the Chinese authorities really have your air crew – they've denied it vehemently."

"That's my concern."

"Pardon me, I think if you're going to start a full-scale nuclear war and claim Pentagon backing that you simply don't have, then it is everyone's concern."

"Now hold on," the Vice President said, taking a step backwards. "What's that about the Pentagon? And we've not actually decided…"

But Ardman wasn't going to be interrupted. "In fact, what have you done? Apart from a knee-jerk reaction that got your own men killed or injured." Ardman's lips curled slightly. "I use the word 'jerk' deliberately."

Wilson's face was turning a shade of purple and he looked like he might burst.

"But no," Ardman went on, "you'd rather persuade a weak-minded, xenophobic Vice President to take matters into his own hands and lead us to the brink of Armageddon than work to make sure these madmen – whoever they are – are stopped before they can launch so much as a firecracker. So much for proportional reasoned response. And you dare to lecture us about intelligence?"

Despite the situation, Chance felt himself start to smile.

Colonel Wilson, however, was not seeing the humour in Ardman's accusation and sarcasm.

"You know nothing about what's really happening here!" he roared.

"So enlighten me. What do you know about what's going on in the White House? Why are you lying about Pentagon intelligence? How are you *really* involved?"

For a moment it looked like the General would reply. But then he blinked and seemed to gather himself. "Get these men out of here," he ordered. "Out of my sight, and out of the security area. They are no longer welcome. That clear?"

Ardman and Chance were marched from the truck and escorted out of the cordon.

"That went well," said Chance.

"As well as I expected," Ardman agreed. "Wilson won't find it so easy to persuade the Vice President to authorise an attack now."

"And what's Wilson up to? Is he involved?"

"Oh, yes. He can't simply be that monumentally stupid, pig-headed and spoiling for a fight. Have you seen the latest trade figures between the US and China? The US unemployment projections? With that and the missing air crew, I think he believes the two countries are already at war. And he's willing to bend the rules so he can get in the first strike."

"Kill or be killed. Destroy their economy before they destroy ours."

"Something like that."

"And Marshal Wieng and Colonel Shu?"

"They both have their own reasons for wanting to threaten or even attack China. I'll get on to the Pentagon, and play them the recording of Wilson talking to the Vice President. But even with General Wilson muzzled there's a very serious situation developing here to say the least."

"Don't I know it," said Chance, looking past the security cordon, the military vehicles and the troops to the White House. "And Rich and Jade are still in there somewhere."

There wasn't time to hide. The door clicked open, and a figure stepped into the secure room.

Jade leaped up from the sofa, startled but ready to make a run for it.

The woman in the doorway was Kate Hunter. "Hi, Jade. Chuck managed to let me know you were here."

"What's going on?" Jade demanded. "Who are those guys, and where have they taken Rich and Chuck and the President?" She felt the tears welling up. "They killed Dex! What do they want?"

Kate glanced round nervously. "Hold on, hold on. Halford's OK. Well, a bit groggy – he was hit with a tranquiliser dart."

Jade gave a gasp of surprise and relief. "Oh, thank God. Are you sure he's OK?"

"The plan was to tranquilise the President, but thankfully things didn't all go to plan. Halford will be fine. Or as fine as any of us in this mess."

"You mean you are working with them?!" Jade exclaimed. "I saw you with that creepy guy in the orchestra."

"Jefferson Kent. Creepy is about right. Yes, I was working with them. Undercover, as part of my job. We thought they were planning to kidnap a senator who's sympathetic to free trade with China. Seems they've stepped up a gear or two."

"But what do they want?"

"They're convinced we need to retrench: buy American goods, protect people's jobs. The President abandoning those captured airmen to the Chinese was the last straw as they see it. Maybe they have a point, but this isn't the way to make it. And now Marshal Wieng and Colonel Shu are here."

"I heard," said Jade. "I think Marshal Wieng locked me in."

"Him or Kent. Not deliberately, they just smashed the entry coder off the wall so the locking mechanism was bust. I had to re-attach the wires to get the door open.

"But what are they *doing*?"

"They want to threaten Beijing. Give Wiengwei independence, or they launch a nuclear attack. Add in the safe return of the air crew, some trade agreements and an undertaking not to undercut American manufacturing and take US imports, and Kent and his cronies are happy too."

"Everyone's a winner," said Jade sarcastically.

"Yeah, right. Except Beijing will never agree. And Marshal Wieng is just the sort of megalomaniac who'll launch the nukes anyway. If he can get the codes from the President. He'll probably never even give them a chance to accede to his demands."

"So what do we do?"

Kate Hunter sighed. "I need to get back. Kent's suspicious of me anyway, which is why I haven't been able to do anything. If they'd give me a gun I could take them all out. But armed with bits of cello and a piece of a saxophone that only fires tranquiliser darts, I've no hope. But there's something *you* can do."

"Yes?"

Kate leaned close to Jade. "Here's something not many people know – certainly not Kent and Wieng…"

Jade's eyes widened as Kate told her the plan.

The metal briefcase containing the nuclear launch codes was still on the table in the Roosevelt Room where Kent had put it earlier. Standing round it were Kent himself, Marshal Wieng, Colonel Shu, Hank, Chuck White and the President.

Secret Service agent Steve was still sitting in the chair, his wrist still chained to the handle of the case. But now he was conscious, looking round warily for any opportunity to make a move against the gunmen. But there was none.

Kent and Hank had machine pistols aimed at Chuck and the President.

"It's quite simple," said Marshal Wieng. "I want you to open the case. Then I want you to input your authorisation codes, and target a nuclear missile at coordinates I shall supply. It's an area in eastern China. Not a very populated area, so it will do for a warning shot. Just the one missile, that's all. For now. Then I'll issue my demands."

The President shook his head. "I won't do it. I'll never

do it. There is nothing you can threaten that will make me do it."

"Yet you gave yourself up to save a boy's life," Kent rasped. "You'll do it. Even if we have to kill every one of our hostages. Right here in front of you. One by one."

There was movement at the side of the room and Kent spun round. "Where have you been?" he demanded.

Kate Hunter shrugged. "Just checking. I couldn't find Tony."

"Probably taking a leak," Hank said. "Or stepped out for a cigarette. This place is no smoking, right?" he grinned. No one else laughed.

Kent had turned his gun so it was pointing at Kate. "I don't want you wandering off. I want you right here where I can see you. I'm still not sure about you."

"I'm here, aren't I?" said Kate, exasperated. "What do I have to do to prove myself to you?"

Marshal Wieng had been watching the exchange with interest. "You have to kill the first hostage," he said. He turned to Colonel Shu. "Go with her. Bring in the first two hostages, and we shall see if the President is really as resolved as he claims."

"You saved his life once," Kent told the President. "You going to do it again? The first to die will be that boy. Him and one other. But not our friends from the Chinese Embassy, not yet. We'll save them for later. I don't care who else you choose, just bring them here. Now."

20

One of the gunmen shoved Rich into the room where the hostages were being held and shouted across to the woman with cropped hair.

"Another one for you, Marcie."

"The more the merrier," she called back. "Make yourself at home, kid."

Rich quickly scanned the room. He tried to make it seem like he was lost and confused, choosing a place on the floor at random. But when he sat down and pulled his knees up under his chin, he was next to Dex Halford.

"Sorry," Rich murmured.

"No worries. Can't be helped," Halford murmured in response. "We'll bide our time…"

Rich looked round at the other hostages. There looked

like nearly fifty people crammed into the room. All of them looked tired and scared. He knew how they felt. There had been some muttering and whispering when Rich was brought in, but the woman who seemed in charge of the other two gunmen in the room shouted for silence. She got it.

The silence was broken by the arrival of Colonel Shu and Kate Hunter. They spoke quietly to Marcie, and then Kate strode across to where Rich was sitting.

But before Kate could speak, one the Chinese men got to his feet and spouted a torrent of angry invective at Colonel Shu.

She answered him in the same Chinese dialect, brandishing her gun. The Chinese man glared at her for several long moments before he sat down again.

"His time will come," said Colonel Shu to Marcie. "Very soon."

"You – on your feet," Kate snapped at Rich. She nudged him with her foot. She looked at the two Chinese men sitting further away before, both glaring now at Kate. Then she turned back to Halford. "You too. Up you get. Come with me."

"Where are we going?" Rich asked. He didn't have to pretend to be nervous, even though he was sure that Kate must be somehow working to get them free.

"You'll find out," she snapped. Unseen by the gunmen or Colonel Shu, she winked.

Colonel Shu was watching Rich carefully as Kate led him and Halford to the door. "You were at the hospital in England. What are you doing here?"

Rich looked away. He braced himself for the blow, but Colonel Shu had turned and was gesturing for them to walk ahead of her. "It is of no importance," she decided. "This way."

They followed Kate out of the room and along the corridor. Colonel Shu stayed close behind them, with her gun at the ready. As they reached the end of the corridor and turned towards the Roosevelt Room, Kate stopped and held up her hand, frowning.

"Wait, Colonel Shu!" Her voice was an urgent whisper.

Shu pushed past Rich and Halford. "What is it?"

Kate did not reply. Instead she grabbed the machine pistol Shu was holding and wrenched it away from her.

But Shu held on tight, twisting it back towards Kate. Her foot lashed out, catching Kate in the midriff and forcing her away. Kate doubled up, letting go of the gun. Colonel Shu aimed, her finger tightening on the trigger.

Then Rich slammed into her, knocking Shu sideways;

the gun went flying. Rich scrambled to his feet, but Shu was already in a karate stance. Her foot whipped out again, catching Rich on the chest. He staggered back and tried to parry the savage jabbing of Shu's tensed hands.

Kate aimed a punch at Shu, but it was parried easily. Kate kicked out, but Shu grabbed the grey material of her suit trousers and spun her round, pushing her away. Kate fell to the floor and Shu continued her relentless attack on Rich.

Rich backed away, looking for an opportunity to punch back. But he was fighting a losing battle, and barely able to stay on his feet. Then suddenly, Colonel Shu took a flying leap, but not at Rich – past him, towards the fallen gun. She landed, rolled, collected the machine pistol and was upright again in a single fluid movement.

Her mismatched eyes were filled with anger as she aimed the gun at Kate.

"You traitor." Shu shoved Rich aside. She glanced at Halford, but he was standing absolutely still, his hands behind his back. He was obviously no threat.

Colonel Shu stood between Rich and Halford, aiming the gun at Kate. Her mouth twisted into a smile.

A smile that froze as Halford brought his hands from

behind his back. He pressed the gun that Rich had given him to the side of Colonel Shu's head.

Shu let Kate take the machine pistol from her. Then in a blur of sudden motion, she turned quickly, pivoting on one heel and struck out at Halford.

Except he was no longer there. He had already taken a step to one side, anticipating the attack. With Colonel Shu unbalanced and confused he stepped towards her again. In a quick, easy movement, he tossed the handgun in the air. As Colonel Shu watched the gun in surprise, Halford clenched his now-empty hand into a fist and thumped her hard across the chin.

Colonel Shu dropped to the floor. Halford opened his hand and caught the gun.

"That'll teach you to show off."

"We need to lock her up somewhere," said Rich.

"It'll have to be pretty secure," Halford pointed out.

"I know just the place," said Kate. "Snip a wire, and there's no way she can get out."

The military ambulance was only metres outside the cordon when the man in a suit flagged it down. He waved his ID at the driver so fast, he had no time to read it.

"We need a couple of minutes with the patient; I hope that's all right."

Before the driver could answer he heard the back doors of the ambulance open, and surprised voices from inside.

"No, sir, it is not all right." But the man had already walked away, and the driver jumped out of the ambulance to follow.

The back doors were open and two men were talking quickly and earnestly with the patient. A paramedic was trying to usher them out again, but with no success.

"I'm sorry, sir," the driver said. "I'll get rid of them."

"No, wait," said the patient. He was propped up on a gurney, a drip attached to the back of his hand and his leg strapped and bandaged. "These guys saved my life. Give us a couple of minutes, OK?"

He smiled at Chance and Ardman.

"So what can I do for you gentlemen?" Roberts asked as soon as he was alone with the British intelligence officers.

"You are the commander who's been given authority to enter the White House and rescue the President," said Ardman. "And as far as I'm aware that order hasn't been rescinded. We want you to take over the infiltration again."

Roberts gave a short laugh. "Hey, I'm wounded, here. And my team is shot to hell. Only Al and Barney are left. They're good, but they're not that good. Anyway, my loyalty is to the United States of America."

"Then help us to save its President," Ardman said. "My hands are tied unless I can get official clearance. If you second my people to your unit, and if you command the operation, we can do the job."

Roberts pointed at his leg. "I'm not commanding anything like this."

"We'll get you linked in," Chance told him. "Full video and radio link. The team leader will have operational command of course, but you make the Go – No go decision."

"What do you say?" Ardman asked. "You know how critical the timing is. Those maniacs in there could have access to the launch procedures any time."

"That's their plan? You're kidding."

Ardman shook his head. "I wish we were."

Roberts' head flopped back on the narrow pillow. "OK, say I did give you the authority, who are these people you reckon can pull off a rescue from one of the most secure buildings on the planet?"

"The only people who could, apart from maybe your

own team. They're ready and waiting. They've got floor plans and security details, and they've even marked out the floor layout in a hangar I borrowed over at Dulles Airport," Ardman said. "They've been planning and training since they arrived yesterday. The SAS."

Roberts drew in a deep breath. "You're a very convincing man, Mr Ardman."

"Thank you."

"But your SAS team still lack what we needed. They have no idea what's really going on inside the White House. They'd need to know the number and positions of gunmen, how well armed and trained they are, where the hostages are being kept, what support we might have once inside… You convince me you know even half of that, and you're in business. But I don't know how you're going to find it out."

"I do," a voice said from the back of the ambulance. "You can ask me."

A female figure was silhouetted in the open doors. She wore a torn dress that had been pale blue but was now stained with mud.

"Jade?!" said Chance in amazement. "How the hell did you get here?"

21

Marshal Wieng nodded to Kent. "It's time at last. Now you can open the case."

Grinning, Kent leaned across Steve and pressed the button-catches by the clasps holding the metal briefcase closed. Nothing happened. He tried again, but the raised buttons didn't move. They didn't press in or slide or turn.

Wieng drew a deep, impatient breath. "Open it," he said to Steve.

The man shook his head. "I can't."

"I said, *open it*." Wieng brought up his gun and pressed it hard against the side of Steve's head.

"Can't you see he's telling the truth?" said the President. "The case doesn't open. Not for him, not for anyone. Not without an electronic key that you don't have."

Wieng jolted the end of the gun viciously into Steve's head, knocking him aside. He aimed at the briefcase.

"No!" Kent rasped. "You'll damage the launch station. They're just trying to make us angry so we'll make a mistake. Wait for the hostages. Then they'll open it."

Wieng was still breathing heavily, but he lowered the gun. "You are right. We have plenty of time. China is going nowhere. It will still be there when we launch."

"Though it won't be soon afterwards," said Kent.

The paramedic wasn't happy, but he fixed Captain Roberts up as best as he could, telling him more than once that he should be in hospital.

"You've lost a lot of blood, and when the painkillers start to wear off, you'll know about it."

"I'll leave when the President does," Roberts told him. "Not before."

He made a couple of quick calls on the driver's cell phone. The first was to the Pentagon, where he spoke to a woman he knew only as 'Broker'. She assured him that what Ardman had said was true and that 'things' were 'happening'. She also gave him a codeword he needed to identify himself to the Quartermaster at a military depot in Maryland.

The Quartermaster, Staff Sergeant Johnson, took down the list of equipment that Roberts asked for.

"That all?"

Roberts gave a short laugh. "It'll do."

"It had better. You guys aiming to start a war or something?"

"Aiming to stop one," Roberts replied.

"You'll put me out of business," Johnson said. But neither of them laughed at that.

By the time Roberts snapped the cell phone shut, Al and Barney were standing at the end of the gurney.

"So this is for real?" said Al.

"You know the situation."

Barney said, "We've just got back from Dulles. Those guys have a pretty neat set up. They've got plans and schematics, a whole mock-up of the West Wing with lines painted on the hanger floor to show where the walls are. They know their stuff."

"They want helicopters," Roberts said. "They know they can't get in from the roof, don't they?"

Al nodded. "Yup."

"So what happens next?" Barney asked.

The answer came from behind him. Ardman was standing at the back door of the ambulance. "If Captain

Roberts has organised the equipment we need, then we just have to wait for the Pentagon to sort out the small matter of the chain of command."

"Could take a while," Roberts warned. "If General Wilson doesn't agree, which he won't, things could get sticky."

"Which is why we aren't going to wait. If your two colleagues here would like to come with me, I have a little treat in store for them."

Al and Barney looked at Roberts, who nodded as best he could while lying in the narrow bed. "What did you have in mind?"

Ardman smiled. "Mr Chance and Jade are going to give your friends a tour of the White House. Or at least, some of the parts of it that are not on the plans you were given. Get your guns, as they say, and we'll be on our way."

Rich and Halford were pushed into the Roosevelt Room by Kate Hunter, their hands tied behind their backs. Kate was carrying Colonel Shu's machine pistol.

Rich didn't have to act much to look suitably scared.

There were two gunmen in the room, as well as Wieng and Kent. One of them had Chuck at gunpoint; the other was standing smirking, holding a Secret Service handgun. Apart from the President himself, the only other person in the room was Secret Service agent Steve, his wrist still attached to the briefcase by a heavy metal chain.

The President turned as they entered. He looked tired and drawn. Marshal Wieng, by contrast, was elated. Kent frowned as he saw that Kate was alone, and had a gun.

"I told you Tony was missing," she said. "Colonel Shu's gone to check what's happening."

"Without her gun?" said Kent. "Looks to me like *you've* got it."

"I needed it to secure these hostages. Anyway, she's got a handgun."

Kent frowned, but he seemed satisfied with the explanation. He turned back to the President, standing beside the briefcase. "Last chance, Mr President."

"You know my answer," said the President.

"This is going to be a long day," Kent told him. "But if that's how it has to be…" He turned to Marshal Wieng. "I guess we do this the hard way."

"So it would seem. Mr President – open the briefcase."

The President glanced at Rich, and then looked away. "I can't."

Marshal Wieng patted the President on the shoulder,

as if he was consoling a friend. "Of course you can't." He turned to Kate. "Kill them."

She raised the gun.

Everything was a sudden blur. Rich had the makeshift tranquiliser gun that Kate had assembled. He brought it from behind his back, and fired straight at the gunman covering Chuck.

The gunman stared in surprise at the dart sticking out of his chest. As the man collapsed, Chuck wrenched his gun from him and brought it round in a swift arc that connected with the chin of the second gunman.

But the second gunman reeled back just as Halford produced his handgun and fired at him. The bullet missed. The gunman fired his own pistol, but without time to take aim the bullets went wide.

Rich dived for cover.

Marshal Wieng grabbed the President and positioned him as a shield before Kate could fire.

Kent also reacted quickly. He had the metal briefcase and thrust it into Steve's hands, jamming his gun into the man's face. Halford stepped forward, bringing his handgun to bear on Kent.

The gunman Halford had missed was still firing, getting his aim now. A bullet grazed past Kate's ear, and she responded with a rapid burst of fire. The man was slammed back across the table.

But he was thrown between Kent and Halford. Halford moved to one side as quickly as his false leg would allow. But he wasn't quick enough to stop Kent dragging Steve to his feet. Now Kent was behind Steve, the gun still jammed in the man's neck.

Marshal Wieng was also backing away with the President.

"It's over," Chuck yelled at them. "Give yourselves up now, while you still can."

But as Wieng and Kent backed from the room into the corridor, they could all hear the shouts from deep within the White House. In moments, more of Kent's team would arrive – and Rich knew he and his friends would be outnumbered.

Meanwhile, Wieng was getting away with the President, and Kent had Steve and the Football. With both of them, Marshal Wieng could launch the US nuclear missiles.

Wieng fired suddenly. A burst of shots that ripped into the floor by Chuck's feet. He dived to one side, unable to fire back in case he hit the President. Kate returned fire – but it was a warning only, hammering harmlessly into the ceiling.

Wieng had dragged the President out into the corridor. Kent, gun at Steve's neck, backed out after him. The worst thing about it was the man's smile. He'd won and he knew it.

With no chance at all of a clear shot, there was nothing that Halford or Chuck or Kate could do. Only Rich could stop them now. He took aim, swallowed as he tried not to think how important this moment was, and fired. It was the only thing he could do.

He shot Steve.

22

The dart struck Steve in the upper leg, and the Secret Service agent slumped immediately. Kent stared at Rich in disbelief. He grabbed Steve round the chest, struggling to keep him upright, but the unconscious man was a dead weight. He slid to the floor, leaving Kent exposed.

Immediately, both Kate and Chuck opened fire.

Kent dived back behind the doorway. Rich heard him cry out and guessed he'd been hit. Halford hurried to check on Steve's unconscious body. Kate and Chuck were out into the corridor, guns at the ready.

"Help me with him," Halford told Rich. "We can't leave him here. We'll have to carry him." He glanced up at Rich. "But yes – good one."

"Thanks."

Together they lifted the man, and Halford hooked his arm under the chain attached to the Football briefcase. They staggered out into the corridor.

Kate and Chuck had taken cover in alcoves on opposite sides. Chuck fired a burst along the corridor as someone appeared at the other end. They quickly moved back round the corner.

"We can't stay here," said Kate. "We're almost out of ammunition."

"And it won't take them long to send someone round to come at us from behind," Halford pointed out. "We can't defend ourselves from both directions."

"Oval Office," Chuck called back to them. "It's where I tried to get the President before. We'll be safe in there."

Chuck and Kate gave covering fire as Rich and Halford half carried, half dragged Steve across the corridor. The Oval Office was only a few metres away, but it seemed to take forever. As soon as they were inside, they dumped him on a sofa near the door.

Halford hurried back to the door. "I'll cover you, move!"

Kate and Chuck ran for the doorway as Halford stepped into the corridor and fired his pistol rapidly.

Bullets smashed into the door frame as the gunmen at the other end returned fire.

Then more gunfire – this time from the other direction. The carpet at Halford's feet exploded and he dived out of the way of the line of bullets that ripped across the doorway.

Chuck stepped forward, firing rapidly. Then his gun clicked on empty and he was forced to step back into the room.

Unable to get back through the door, Halford took cover in an alcove. He loosed off several more shots before his gun, too, was out of ammunition.

"We have to help him!" Rich shouted above the gunfire. He ran to the door.

But Chuck grabbed him and pulled him back. "It's too late. I'm sorry."

Several of Kent's team were advancing down the corridor. Marcie – the woman who had been supervising the hostages – had her gun trained on Halford. He raised his hands in defeat. But his expression was defiant as he glanced quickly at Rich and Chuck.

Then Chuck was slamming the door shut and operating an electronic lock. There was a heavy *thunk* as deadbolts shot into place. The bullets hitting the door sounded like hailstones on a thin roof.

"Will it hold?" Rich asked. But he was more worried about what would happen to Halford, and where Jade was, than about himself.

"Oh yes," said Kate. "It's designed to withstand quite a blast. The windows too."

"There are agents permanently on duty on the roof, with stinger missiles to shoot down any incoming helicopters or planes," Chuck explained. "But if an attacker got off a missile, this office would take the hit and not even need repainting."

Steve was still out cold on the sofa.

The office was just as Rich had expected. He'd seen it in photographs and on TV and films. The enormous presidential seal on the carpet, the two sofas between the main door and the desk – the famous wooden desk made from timbers from the Victorian British ship HMS Resolute. There was another door to an outer office, and Chuck was sealing that too.

"We'll be fine in here. No one can get in."

"Yes," said Rich. "But we can't get out. We're trapped."

Kate and Chuck exchanged looks, and to Rich's surprise they smiled.

"You reckon?" said Chuck.

*

Jade was glad she'd had time to change out of her dress into combat gear. Barney had sent someone to find her camouflage trousers and a green t-shirt. She was especially glad to lose her shoes. The army boots were loose, even though she'd laced them as tight as she could. But she had made this same journey in high heels, and it wasn't an experience she was keen to repeat.

She'd made it clear she didn't want to be offered a gun – she was sure she'd never use it even if she knew how. Jade was beginning to wish she'd turned down the bullet-proof vest as well. It was stiff and uncomfortable, but she knew wearing it might save her life.

A couple of hours ago, she had made the journey in the dark, alone and uncertain of where she was going or what she'd find at the other end. This time she was not alone, and all four of them had torches.

The light picked out the crumbling brickwork of the curved walls, the uneven floor with its dark pools of standing water. Cobwebs hung like ragged curtains, and rats scuttled in the shadows. Jade was so glad she hadn't been able to see them before. She had heard them, though, just as she had listened to the drip-drip of the condensation falling into the puddles and distant, muffled sound of traffic and sirens above.

And she had almost cried with relief when she saw light seeping round the heavy metal doorway. The bolts had been rusted stiff, and her relief became frustration as she struggled to slide them back. But she had managed, and emerged blinking through a concealed door into the back of a small outhouse full of gardening equipment on the edge of Lafayette Park, just across Pennsylvania Avenue from the White House grounds to the north.

The biggest stroke of luck had been arriving at the military cordon in time to spot Ardman and Dad flagging down an ambulance.

It seemed ages ago. Since then, she'd told Ardman, Dad and Captain Roberts everything she knew about the situation in the White House – what she'd seen for herself, and what Kate had told her. And now here she was, going back. She must be mad, she thought. But she knew she had no option. Dad knew it too – he'd only made a token attempt to talk her out of it, but Jade knew what the bad guys looked like, she knew the layout of the place, and she knew that Rich was in there somewhere. She had no choice.

"Not far now," said Jade. She remembered rounding this corner, and scraping her ankle on what must have been that pile of fallen stones from the tunnel roof.

"Lucky we've got you," said Al.

"Yeah," Barney agreed. "This tunnel isn't marked on any of the plans I've seen."

"It was built as a secret escape route for the President, decades ago. That's what Kate Hunter told me. So I guess that's why it's not on the plans. It starts in the Oval Office, leads down between some of the basement rooms, then out across the White House lawn."

"OK, let's take a minute," said Chance. "I'll go in first when we get there. Jade, you'll come last. If there's any trouble, anything at all, then you run like hell and tell Captain Roberts what's happening. You still getting this, Roberts?"

Jade heard the reply in her earpiece. Robert's voice was punctuated by static and crackles, and he was barely audible.

"Yes, but you're beginning to break up. Any further, and that jamming device they've got will do for the comms. So from here on, you're probably on your own. Your friends just called and said they'd be joining the party soon. We'll give you one hour, and if we don't hear back or get some sort of signal for them to come in, then they'll be joining you anyway."

"Understood. Let's make that exactly one hour from…" Chance checked his watch. "…Now."

Roberts' voice was barely understandable now, there was so much static. "You certain your guys know what they're doing?"

"Absolutely," Chance replied. "It's just *us* I'm not sure about." He slid back the bolt on his machine pistol and released the safety catch. "OK, guys. Let's do it."

Rich was looking right at the portrait of George Washington that dominated the wall of the Oval Office. It was huge, almost life-sized. Chuck and Kate had drawn his attention to it.

"What about it?" he asked. "It's Washington, I know that."

"Maybe this'll surprise you," said Kate. She reached out for the side of the frame, but before her hand reached it, the frame began to move. Kate gave a gasp of astonishment and stepped back.

Chuck raised his gun. "What the hell..? No one should know about this."

The whole picture was moving, swinging out from the wall towards Rich and the others. It was hinged down one side, like a door.

And through the door stepped a figure in dark combat gear. His shape was bulked out with a bullet-proof vest, and he was carrying a machine pistol identical to the ones that Chuck and Kate were holding.

Behind him came two more men in identical gear, also with guns. And behind them Rich could see a smaller, slighter figure he recognised at once.

"You OK, Rich?" John Chance asked. "It's good to see you all again."

Jade pushed through the picture-doorway and grabbed Rich in a tight hug. "You're all right!"

"I was," he said, pulling away. "Now I've got cracked ribs and crush injuries." But he was grinning.

"So what's the situation?" Chance was asking.

"The bad guys have the President, and plan to launch a nuclear attack on China. Meanwhile we're kind of trapped in this one room," Chuck told him.

Chance nodded. Business as usual. "Good job I'm here then. It's time we sorted things out."

23

Wounded and frustrated, Kent was in a foul mood. His arm was caked in blood, but luckily the bullets had both gone right through. The bone was shattered, and he had the arm supported in a sling made from torn-up strips of tablecloth. It hurt like hell, and someone was going to pay.

He had resisted the temptation to shoot Halford as soon as he'd been overpowered. Maybe the man meant something to the President – he was obviously trained and yet he didn't seem to be with the Secret Service. Some British guest who'd been in the wrong place at the wrong time. Kent consoled himself with the thought that he could always shoot him later.

A pleasure deferred was a pleasure increased.

Now he was preparing to vent his fury on another

target. Hank had collected up the grenades the dead Special Forces men had with them. Under Kent's direction he was removing the explosive cores and lining them up along the bottom of the door to the Oval Office.

Kent held the last grenade himself. As soon as Hank had finished, he'd set off the explosives and blow the door down. It might be bullet-proof but he doubted it could withstand such an explosion. Kent could already imagine stepping through the shattered remains of the door and gunning down that traitorous bitch and her colleague – and the kid who'd denied him the Football.

That wouldn't happen again, Kent decided. If he had to hack the man's hand off to get the briefcase back, then he would. He grimaced at a rush of pain in his arm. But he was not hurting as much as his country. And soon they'd both be healed.

"Nearly done," said Hank.

"That's fine," Kent told him. "Those jokers ain't going nowhere. Except maybe to hell."

"We were hoping to sneak in without anyone knowing, and clean up this mess quickly and relatively quietly," said Chance. "Looks like that isn't going to be possible."

"I'm afraid not," Chuck agreed. "Kent will have people

watching that door, waiting for us to make a move."

Chance tried his radio. It gave nothing but static. "Useless."

"They've got some sort of jammer linked into the White House communications network," said Kate. "It blocks out cell phone and radio too. I don't know how it works, but one of Lorraine's jobs was to jam all the radio communications when we arrived, then set it up in the Situation Room downstairs to block the landlines."

"That has to be a priority," Chance decided. "The assault team will need working communications to have the best hope of success."

"Can we get a message to Captain Roberts so they know to focus on the comms?" Barney asked.

"Without a working radio or phone?" Al pointed out.

"We could send someone back down the tunnel with a message. Bring the attack forward too," said Barney.

"You volunteering?" Kate asked.

"I'm not leaving here without the President," Barney told her.

Chance had tuned and was looking at Rich and Jade. They both guessed what was coming next.

"No way," said Jade. "You need me here, remember."

"We've got Chuck and Kate now," Chance told her.

"Still no way."

"And I'm staying too," said Rich quickly. "I need to see this through. To get Dex Halford away from those guys."

"Dex can take care of himself."

"So can we," Rich shot back. "So we stay." He stuffed his hands into his pockets defiantly, and felt something he had forgotten he had. "Anyway, there must be some way round this jamming. Some frequency that works or whatever."

He took out the cell phone he had taken from Steve earlier.

The Secret Service agent was sitting groggily on the sofa, but he stood up when he saw what Rich had. He quickly checked his own pockets.

"Yeah, sorry, Chuck told me to look after it for you," said Rich. "I guess you want it back." He tossed the phone across to Steve, who gave a gasp of horror before managing to catch it.

"You had that all this time?" Chuck asked.

Rich nodded. "But it doesn't get a signal, of course."

Chuck took the phone from Steve. "There is one number it will call. One number it could call from the middle of a nuclear war or the bottom of the sea." He thumbed a sequence of buttons and held the cell phone to his ear.

The call was answered immediately.

"I bet you never thought that phone would ring, Major," said Chuck after he'd given his name and Secret Service number. "Well, don't worry, this isn't what you think. This is the only number I can call and I need you to put me through to the Pentagon Operations Room…" He listened for a few moments, then said: "Yes, Major. This order does come direct from the President himself."

"If the President really was here, we could just walk out down the tunnels," Jade said quietly to Rich.

"More fun this way," said Rich.

While Chuck was talking urgently to the Pentagon, John Chance put an arm round each of his children. "You can both leave now if you want. You don't have to stay. You've done enough. More than enough – both of you."

"We're staying," said Jade.

"But maybe you should send Steve down the tunnel," Rich added. "If they can't get the Football, then at least they can't launch the missiles, no matter what else they do."

"Good idea," said Kate. She hurried over to talk to Steve and helped him to the secret door.

"I'll be OK," he assured her. "I'm just a bit groggy. Good luck, you guys. I'll be waiting for you outside. You want me to take that?" he asked Chuck, pointing to the cell phone.

Chuck considered. "Right now it's the only communication link we have. I'll hang on to it, if that's OK. The bad guys don't know we have it..

Steve nodded, and stepped past the painting and into the escape tunnel. Chuck handed the cell phone to Chance. "They're patching in Captain Roberts. And they've sent a team over to see General Wilson. Would you believe he's not told the Pentagon anything about what's happening here and the only information they have is from Ardman?"

"I'd believe it."

Chuck sucked a deep breath through his teeth. "Well, hopefully we won't be his problem for much longer. And he won't be ours."

Halford stumbled and fell the last few steps. Marshal Wieng hauled him to his feet and shoved him along the corridor.

The President was already in the Situation Room, seated at the conference table. Behind him, a screen showed a distant shot of the military vehicles on Pennsylvania Avenue. The woman with flame-red hair was holding a Secret Service-issue pistol to the President's head.

Halford was shoved into a seat close to the President. He spread his hands on the table. "Good morning, Mr President."

The President nodded. "Not sure what's good about it. But it may get better."

"Silence!" Marshal Wieng shouted. "I haven't yet decided what to do with you. Do you think your military will launch an attack on China to save their President's life?"

The President smiled thinly. "No."

"Then without the Football, there is no point in keeping you alive." He raised his gun.

"If he was going to shoot you, he'd have done it before now," said Halford.

Wieng moved the gun across so it was aimed at Halford. "The President is a useful hostage, you are right. But there's nothing to stop me shooting you, is there?"

"Nothing at all," Halford agreed. "But the more hostages you have the better for you. And you have no idea who I am or even if I'm important. Remember, you can't change your mind if you get it wrong. You can only kill me once."

Wieng's lip curled as he considered this. Marcie came into the room behind him. She was holding two sets of handcuffs.

"I found these in the Secret Service offices," she said. "Thought they might be useful."

"Very useful. Cuff these two to the table legs."

Marcie moved towards the President. "I also found one of our people in there – Tony. He's dead. Someone broke his neck."

Wieng gave a grunt of anger. "Stop," he decided. "I want him to do it." He jabbed the gun at Halford. "Give him the cuffs."

Without comment, Halford took the handcuffs. He leaned to look under the table, and reached past the President to attach one handcuff round a metal support strut between the main legs of the table. He gave it several hard tugs to show it was secure and the strut would hold. "Happy?"

Wieng nodded. "I am still hoping that Mr Kent can recover the Football. So you'll forgive me if I keep you both alive for the moment. I may indeed have need of you."

The handcuff was not long enough to reach up to the top of the table, so Halford attached it to the President's lower leg. He snapped the cuff shut, and the President grimaced as he felt it tight on his ankle.

"Sorry, sir," Halford murmured.

Marshal Wieng motioned to the red-haired woman. "Lorraine, check it is secure."

She examined the cuffs and pulled again to make sure the strut was solid. It was – there was no way that the President could pull it free of the table. She took the second set of handcuffs and attached one end to the equivalent strut on the other side of the table.

Halford moved round to be close enough. "Allow me," he said, taking the free end of the handcuffs and snapping it closed round his own ankle. "Happy with that?"

The woman glanced at the closed handcuffs to check they were secure. "That's fine. He's not going anywhere."

"So, any chance of breakfast?" Halford asked.

Wieng slammed the butt of his gun into Halford's face, knocking him sideways.

"Guess that's a no," said Halford, rubbing his bruised cheek.

Then from above them came the sound of a massive explosion. Halford felt the room shake. For a moment he thought that help had arrived.

But then Wieng said: "Don't worry. That's merely Mr Kent amusing himself."

Even in the Roosevelt Room, which was well away from the Oval Office door, Kent felt the thump of the blast wave against his chest. Smoke billowed down the corridor. Kent and Hank stepped back into the corridor, ready to fire at anything that moved. Kent now had a pistol that he could use one-handed. He trained it on the thinning smoke.

But as the corridor cleared, he could see that the door to the Oval Office was still there. The wood had been stripped away to reveal the armour plate beneath. It was battered and scorched, but intact. Enraged, Kent strode towards the door, determined to kick it down if he had to.

Hank grabbed his good arm, holding him back. "Careful. The floor's gone – look."

Sure enough, the corridor ended in a ragged mess of carpet and wooden floorboards. Dust and smoke rose from the hole. Kent gave another cry of rage and frustration. He turned to go, but then he saw something that made him stop. Something in the clearing smoke and falling dust and debris. Something beneath the floor.

Hank had seen it too. "There's a hole. Like a tunnel or something down there."

If it was a tunnel, it was blocked now by the fallen rubble from the explosion above. But that was not what changed Kent's mood from anger to elation. Lying at the bottom of the hole was a man. He was unconscious, a livid bruise darkening on his forehead where he'd been hit by falling debris he'd been too groggy to avoid.

Grimy but undamaged, the metal briefcase attached to the man's wrist gleamed as it caught the dust-filtered light.

24

As the door to the mobile HQ was pulled open, General Wilson looked up. He was still trying to persuade the Vice President of the best course of action. He got to his feet, pointing down the length of the vast truck.

"Who let that joker back inside the cordon?" he bellowed. "Get him out of here."

"That's not very hospitable," Ardman called back as two soldiers hurried to restrain him. "Especially as I've brought guests."

The soldiers hesitated, then stepped aside as two more people stepped up into the truck. One was in uniform; the other wore a plain but expensive dark suit.

"General Sanchez, sir!" Wilson saluted, unable to disguise his astonishment.

"Wilson," Sanchez replied, saluting back. "I don't think you know Mr Smith from the Pentagon."

"Mr Smith?"

"It will do for the moment," replied the man. "Mr Vice President, sir," he went on, "there's a car ready to take you to the Pentagon where you are required to chair a meeting with the Secretaries of State, Defense, and Homeland Security."

The Vice President was looking pale and confused. "I thought the Secretary of State was in the Middle East."

"Well, perhaps you'll have a short wait for her return," said Mr Smith. "At the Pentagon."

The Vice President swallowed. He barely glanced at Wilson or Ardman. It was clear he had met Mr Smith before and knew exactly who he really was. "Of course. I'll, er, leave you to it."

"That would be best, sir," General Sanchez agreed. "Now, Wilson, you got somewhere private we can talk for a minute. Mr Ardman has filled us in on what's been happening and I'd like to hear how you're responding. I gather Captain Roberts has been authorised to use any means necessary to ensure the safety of the President. I'm hoping you're going to tell me that's still the case. Am I right?" He followed General Wilson to the conference area at the back of the truck.

Ardman and Chance hung back.

"Not going along to see the fireworks?" Mr Smith asked quietly.

"I'll let you wash your dirty laundry in private," said Ardman.

"With respect, that is completely unacceptable, *sir*." General Wilson's angry shout echoed round the headquarters.

"Or as privately as you can," said Ardman.

"I've given Sanchez five minutes to talk the General round. After that it's my turn. I'll play him back his conversation with the Vice President and ask some pertinent questions about where this incontrovertible Pentagon intelligence came from. That ought to persuade Wilson to hand over command without any trouble."

"If it doesn't, you may have to shoot him," said Ardman, with the flicker of a smile.

"I may indeed," said Smith.

He didn't sound like he was joking.

It took less than twenty minutes for General Wilson to hand over command to General Sanchez and agree that Captain Roberts was still authorised to take whatever action he deemed necessary to rescue the President. Not that he had a lot of choice. General Sanchez outranked Wilson anyway, but without Wilson's willing cooperation, things could become difficult. While it was damning, Ardman's recording of Wilson wasn't absolute proof of treachery.

Captain Roberts, his leg now properly strapped up and the intravenous drip no longer necessary, had graduated from his stretcher to a wheelchair. Two soldiers lifted it into the headquarters truck, where a workstation had been prepared.

"The only direct contact we have at the moment is a voice link to Agent White," General Sanchez said. "I'm getting it patched through."

"As soon as we find someone who knows what frequency he's using to broadcast, then we can use that for the whole team," Roberts pointed out.

"Trouble is, the device he's using broadcasts on an awful lot of frequencies. We're trying to isolate the one that's getting through to the network relays," Sanchez told him. "Shouldn't take long, but it isn't one of the usual channels."

Mr Smith was talking on his cell phone. He gestured to one of the technicians close by, and she leaned across and flipped a switch on the control desk in front of Roberts.

Immediately, Chuck White's voice came loud and clear through nearby speakers: "...was hoping you could send more people along the escape tunnel, but it's blocked off now."

"This is Ardman," Ardman replied, "Captain Roberts is now in charge of this operation, and is on the line. It sounds as if things are happening at your end."

"They are getting kind of urgent. Any news of the helicopters yet?"

"General Sanchez here. There are obviously problems sanctioning the use of the SAS on American soil. But I don't think we have any choice. Wilson's compromised, and I'm not going to risk using any of his people on this. Roberts and his guys are the only others available and they're already in play. Getting a team of Marines here from Quantico is possible, but then they would need to be briefed and of course they haven't trained for this. It would just take too long."

"So what's the deal?" Chuck asked.

"The deal is that Captain Roberts is in charge, so he gets to decide what he wants to do. And if that includes commandeering help from outside his immediate chain of command, I am not going to override the commander in the field."

Ardman had his own cell phone out. "Captain Roberts?"

Roberts nodded. "Like the General says, we don't have a lot of choice. Your team will please consider themselves part of the US military under my direct command."

"They'll love that." Ardman pressed a speed dial button. His call was answered immediately. "Yes please," he said quietly into the phone. "Code name: Eagle." He snapped the phone shut. "They're all yours, Captain Roberts."

Before Ardman had finished speaking, the four screens in front of Roberts snapped into life. One showed a general view of an airbase. Three black helicopters started to lift into the air, angular brutal shapes against the morning sky.

The other screens showed views from inside each of the helicopters. There were six black-clad men in each, faces masked behind respirators. Assault rifles held ready.

One of the men gave a thumbs-up. His voice came through the speakers, filtered through his mask: "Hawk One to Eagle Control, we are in the air. Flight time to target nest: seven minutes. We need a Go – No go in five.

After that we will be visible to the Magpies and must commit."

"Understood," Roberts replied. "Go – No-go in five or less. The skies are clear. The military here and the Secret Service on the White House roof have been briefed and will ensure safe passage to the nest."

"That's a relief. Thank you, Eagle. We have just received the alternate frequency channel. Switching to that now."

The female technician leaned over again to adjust another control. "We just got the channel through from the Pentagon. That should work even within the jamming radius."

"Thanks."

Ardman clasped Roberts on the shoulder. "Good luck," he said quietly.

"Seconded," Sanchez agreed.

"I'd wish you luck too," Smith murmured. "If I was really here."

On the main monitor, the helicopters were black dots disappearing into the distance. The image switched to a view of the White House.

"Time to target nest now six minutes."

"You getting this, Agent White?" Roberts asked.

"Loud and clear. Tell them we'll warm the place up for them."

In the Oval Office, Chuck turned to the others. "You ready?"

John Chance was checking his machine pistol. "Ready."

The two American Special Forces soldiers, Al and Barney, nodded.

"Always," said Kate Hunter.

Rich nodded. He looked pale.

Jade swallowed, her throat suddenly dry. "Ready."

It was probably her imagination, but Jade thought she could already hear the approaching thump of the helicopters.

25

There was a side door from the Oval Office that led into the President's secretary's office. From here, there was access into the Cabinet Room and from there another armoured door opened back into the main corridor.

"So far all their attention has been on the main door. I'm hoping they don't even realise we can get out this way," said Chuck.

"Unless they're waiting for us," said Chance.

"We'll give covering fire," Barney told them. "You guys make for the stairs."

"Just to reiterate," Chance told them all. "We don't know where they've taken the President. Kate, Al, Barney – you make for the hostages. The SAS will also be heading that way as you know, so you will support them. Chuck and I will make for the Situation Room. From there we can stop the jamming and more importantly unseal the doors."

"And what about us?" Rich asked.

"You want us to stay here?" said Jade. For once, she was inclined to agree to keep out of trouble.

It was Chuck who replied. "We want you to get to the Secret Service operations room and monitor what's happening."

Chuck gave Agent Steve's cell phone to Rich. "You're through direct to Captain Roberts. Tell him anything he needs to know. Anything you can. He'll have voice contact with the assault team, but he's blind."

Rich took the phone. "Understood."

"And this operations room," said Jade. "How do we get to it?"

"It's hidden," Kate told them. "Concealed so well that even Kent and his guys haven't found it."

"There's a secret door under the stairs," said Rich. "I'll show you." Despite the seriousness of the situation, he couldn't help grinning at Kate and Chuck's look of surprise.

"Hawk One approaching final marker. If you're going to pull the plug this is your last chance."

Captain Roberts glanced at General Sanchez, who gave the slightest nod.

"Understood, Hawk One," said Roberts. "You are Go. I repeat, you are Go."

"Acknowledged. Hawk Two and Three moving to roof. Hawk One standing by."

Roberts leaned forward slightly in his wheelchair. "Get ready, Leopard. Won't be long now."

Out on Pennsylvania Avenue, a massive M1A2 tank stood by the gates to the White House. Its engine idled as it waited for the final order.

In the Situation Room, Steve, who had been pulled from the tunnel, was slumped in a chair beside the President. The metal briefcase was still attached to his wrist, and now lay on the conference table.

"Don't do it, Mr President," said Halford. "No matter what they threaten, don't do it."

Marshal Wieng slammed his fist into Halford's face. "Shut up!"

On the other side of the table, Kent jabbed his machine pistol into the President's cheek. "Tell us how to open it."

He leaned forward, twisting he gun painfully, grinding it into the President's face. The briefcase was coated with dust from the tunnel. As Kent moved, he saw something catch the light – the faintest glimmer on one of the catches.

"What is that?" Kent murmured. He moved the gun from the President's cheek and leaned across. It was an awkward movement with his arm in the sling, and he grunted with pain as he moved.

"What have you found?" Wieng asked.

Lorraine hurried to join Kent. "A sensor," she said. "On the catch." She rubbed at the other catch, to reveal the pale glow. "Wouldn't be visible if it wasn't for the dust."

"Some sort of defence mechanism? A booby trap?" Kent wondered.

Lorraine shook her head. "I think it's a fingerprint scanner."

Kent laughed. "And whose fingerprint do you think it takes to open the case?"

Halford's eyes met the President's, and he knew that Kent had guessed correctly.

There was a noise from outside. It had been growing slowly in volume while all their attention was on the briefcase. But now it was impossible to ignore. On one of the screens at the end of the room, they could see two helicopters approaching the White House. They flew low over the camera and disappeared from sight.

Lorraine ran to the control panel. Another view of the White House flashed up.

"Where are they?" Kent demanded. "Where did they go?"

They all looked up. The noise of the helicopters was still loud above them. But there was no sign of them on the screen.

"There they are," said Lorraine, as the two dark shapes appeared the other side of the White House and flew off into the distance.

"Are they trying to scare us or something?" Kent wondered.

"Go and check everything is OK upstairs," Marshal Wieng told Lorraine. "Let the others know what just happened. Tell them it's nothing, they need to stay calm. And find out where Colonel Shu has got to."

Lorraine took a handgun from the waistband of her trousers and left.

"And you," said Marshal Wieng, pointing at the President, "open the briefcase. Now. Or I will shoot your friend then cut off your thumbs and use them to open it myself." He pressed his gun into the back of Halford's neck.

Al eased open the door from the President's office, just enough to see that the corridor outside was clear. He pushed it open fully, both he and Barney ready to open fire if there was anyone outside.

But the corridor was empty. Kate beckoned for Al and Barney to follow her towards the main door to the Oval Office – the quickest way back to where the hostages were being held.

Chance gestured for Rich and Jade to follow him as he headed the other way, towards the stairs down to the basement. Chuck White followed behind, pulling the door closed behind them, and constantly checking they had not been spotted.

They were almost at the stairs when they ran into trouble. A gunman appeared around the corner of the corridor – heading straight for them.

The sound of the helicopters right above the White House was almost deafening, which was why the gunman who rounded the corner in front of them was looking up at the ceiling, obviously wondering what was happening.

The man caught sight of Chance just as the butt of the gun slammed into his stomach. He doubled over, dropping his own weapon. A second blow left him unconscious on the floor. Chuck ran to help Chance drag the body into a side room.

Alone in the corridor, Rich and Jade froze when Lorraine arrived at the top of the stairs. She raised her pistol in surprise, pointing it right at them.

Rich didn't hesitate. He put his hands up, and tried to look scared – which wasn't too difficult. "Please, don't shoot. Please."

The helicopters seemed to be moving off now, and the woman opened her mouth to reply, but before she could utter a word, the gun was kicked from her hand. She had made the mistake of taking her eyes off Jade for just a second as she was distracted by Rich. Jade's foot slammed into the red-haired woman's wrist.

Lorraine's second mistake was now to turn towards Jade. Rich's fist crashed into her jaw, and she reeled backwards. She stumbled and fell, but she was close to the gun. Her hand closed around it. She sat up, bringing the gun to bear.

John Chance's hand came down in a heavy karate chop on the back of her neck. The woman slumped sideways.

"Let's add her to the collection," said Chance.

The two helicopters paused over the White House for only twenty seconds. Just long enough for the six SAS men inside each chopper to abseil down to the roof. Then they flew on, away over the Potomac River and out of sight.

Two Secret Service agents stood on the roof, watching as the SAS attached ropes to the side rails. One of the SAS men came running over to them.

The agents were standing beside a large open case. Inside was the hand-held surface-to-air missile system that would take out any unauthorised aircraft that tried to approach the White House.

"Good morning," said the black-clad figure.

"Hi," one of the agents replied. "Welcome to the White House. You feeling as useless as we are right now? There's no way into the White House from up here, you know. Else we'd be inside sorting out the bad guys."

The SAS man nodded, and pointed to the missile. "Can I borrow that?"

The agents exchanged looks. "It's only good for ground-to-air, you know. And we'll need authorisation before we can just hand it over," one of them said.

"Fair enough. Do us a favour then, will you?"

"What?"

He pointed at the low concrete stairwell on the other side of the roof. "That's the way down into the West Wing, yes?"

"Yes, but it's sealed off from inside. A dozen hand-grenades won't get through there."

At the edge of the roof, dark figures were preparing to jump out on their ropes. The SAS man checked his watch.

"Hand-grenades might not get through," he agreed. "But a Stinger missile might. And if not, it'll make enough noise to wake the dead and get our chums in there looking the wrong way. So fire on it in twenty-three seconds, please."

He didn't wait for an answer, but walked calmly to the side of the roof and attached his rope.

"Leopard, you may start your run."

The command echoed round the inside of the tank. The driver immediately accelerated along the White House drive. The vehicle had the new LV100-5 engine, which gave it far greater acceleration towards its impressive top speed of 45mph. With the electronic limiter removed, the tank could got even faster – up to

60mph on a paved surface. But speed was not the main consideration today…

Halfway up the drive, the tank turned and started across the main lawn – straight for the West Wing.

"What the hell?" Kent stared at the image on the monitor. "They can't be serious."

"It must be a bluff," Wieng agreed.

The dark shape of a battle tank was heading across the White House lawn, leaving deep tracks behind it in the grass.

Then from above came the sound of a colossal explosion and the whole building juddered.

"See what's happening!" Wieng yelled at Kent. "And start killing the hostages."

Holding his gun in his good hand, Kent ran from the room.

Wieng levelled his own machine pistol at the President. "Play time is over. I am sure there are booby traps that only you know about. So open the case, or I'll shoot you both here and now."

The President held his gaze for a moment, then he looked away, beaten.

"OK," he said. He reached out for the briefcase. As

soon as his thumbs pressed against the clasps, they clicked open. "It's all yours," said the President. "God help us."

Chuck had told Rich how to call up a map of the White House on the main screen in the Surveillance Room. The map showed each room, and the position of every camera together with the key number of that camera.

"This is serious stuff," said Jade, impressed.

She sat next to Rich while he keyed the screens to the cameras in the West Wing.

"Can you hear me?" said Jade into the cell phone. They had agreed she would pass on information while Rich worked the surveillance controls.

"Loud and clear," Captain Robert replied. "What can you tell me?"

"The gunmen are getting excited and nervous since that huge explosion on the roof."

"That was just to keep them on their toes. And looking the other way."

Jade quickly passed on the details of how many gunmen there were in each of the areas as Rich found them on the cameras.

"Then there are three with the hostages and two outside the Oval Office – though Kate, Al and Barney are ready and waiting to deal with them when you start the attack."

There were others in various rooms or patrolling the corridors. Rich pointed out Kent, hurrying to the stairway. They heard him clatter above their heads as he raced upstairs.

On the screen showing the corridor outside the Surveillance Room, Chuck and Chance stepped out of the Secret Service office where they had hidden to let Kent go past. They headed slowly and warily towards the Situation Room.

Another screen showed the scene in the Situation Room itself. "Oh, God," said Rich. "The President has opened the briefcase. I repeat, he's opened the Football."

"Come on, Dad – hurry up!" said Jade.

She held her breath, but it was very clear that Chuck and her dad were not going to be in time to save the President – or to stop those nuclear missiles from being launched…

Marshal Wieng stared at the open briefcase. "What is this?" he demanded. His voice was harsh and angry.

"What does it look like?"

Inside the briefcase was a telephone. An old-fashioned

telephone with a chunky plastic handset resting on a cradle. The main part of the phone had large pushbuttons, and a speaker grille.

"It's a satellite phone," said the President quietly. "Oh, it's pretty old technology now. But it means that the President of the United States can always contact his commanders in the field, or in the air."

Wieng was shaking his head in disbelief. "But – the nuclear codes. The launch instructions. Firing the missiles."

"It's not as easy as that," said the President. "Press a few buttons and destroy the world? In your dreams, Marshal Wieng. These days you have to call up the Joint Chiefs and ask them to initiate the launch. You really think they'll do that for you? Do you?"

Marshal Wieng was shaking with fury. "Then you are no use to me at all."

"None," the President agreed, holding Wieng's entire attention. He leaned back in his chair, the handcuff securing him firmly to the table dug into his lower leg. "So what are you going to do about it? Shoot me?"

"Yes." Marshal Wieng raised his gun. He aimed over the table, taking care to stay well out of Halford's reach. Handcuffed to the table by his leg, just like the President, the man posed no threat at all. No one could stop him now.

Marshal Wieng fired.

26

At the last moment, the huge, heavy tank veered off course. Kent and the two men with him had expected it to crash into the front of the West Wing. They were waiting, guns levelled.

"Told you it was a bluff!" said Kent, his hoarse voice barely audible above the sound of the engines. "They'd never risk killing hostages and the President."

But despite the fact that the tank was now heading away from them, the sound wasn't getting quieter. And it was coming from the other side of the building.

"Decoy!" one of the gunmen realised.

But he was too late.

Hawk One flew low and fast towards the back of the

White House. It barely cleared the trees. As soon as it was over the back lawn, the four black-clad men clinging to the skids let go, and hung beneath the helicopter on ropes.

Two missiles streaked out from the helicopter, detonating moments later against the toughened windows. The glass would resist bullets and even rocket-propelled grenades. But the missiles didn't break the glass – they blew out the whole window frames instead.

Seconds later, Hawk One sped over the roof of the West Wing. It didn't slow down. The four SAS soldiers slammed into the building – two through each of the gaping holes where the windows had been. They released their rope harnesses to land at a run as the ropes were whipped away and up behind them.

They were firing as they entered the building – already clued in by Jade that there were gunmen in each of the rooms they entered.

"Vulture One – gunman down. Press Secretary's office clear. Proceeding."

"Vulture Three – two gunmen down. Annexe clear. Proceeding."

Kent and his men turned at the sound of the twin explosions from the back of the building.

At exactly the same moment, the SAS men on the roof dropped on their ropes. It was the work of seconds to position shaped charges round the window frames, then kick back from the wall as they detonated. The glass was strong enough to survive the blast. But the window frames were not. The soldiers crashed back into the windows, their weight knocking the glass out of the frame and into the room.

Kent whirled round. The man beside him dropped instantly. The other gunman was dead less than two seconds later. Kent dived for the door, one of his falling comrades miraculously shielding his body.

In another room, a woman with a machine pistol saw an SAS man position his charge. The window crashed apart and the man hurled himself into the room. She had him in her sights, an easy kill.

Except the man was burning – his whole body was engulfed in flames. He must have been caught in the explosion. The woman smiled. Let him burn.

It was already too late when she realised that in fact the man was not burning. It was a length of curtain draped over his shoulder that was on fire. The soldier fired and shrugged off the burning blanket in a single easy movement.

"Vulture seven. Gunman down. Room clear, proceeding."

The two gunmen outside the Oval Office turned at the first sounds of the SAS attack. Single aimed shots from behind were enough to take out each of them before they could react.

Kate, Al and Barney moved like shadows along the corridor. Each covered the other's advance as they headed for the room where they knew the hostages were being held. The room that any moment would become a killing ground.

The sound of the explosions from above startled Marshal Wieng. All his attention had been on the President, not on the surveillance screens, or on Dex Halford. But he had already fired. The distraction made no difference.

What did make a difference was Halford.

While Wieng had been concentrating on the President Halford had been working furiously – not on the handcuffs, but on the prosthetic leg they were attached to. It was difficult to undo it through the fabric of his trousers without looking down, without drawing attention to himself.

But he managed just in time.

Halford launched himself along the length of the table just as Marshal Wieng fired his machine pistol. The President remained absolutely still, paper-pale. Halford's arm connected with the barrel of the gun, knocking it sideways. Bullet holes drilled across the wall behind the President.

Wieng gave a roar of anger. He swung the gun viciously, slamming it into Halford and knocking him to the floor. Marshal Wieng looked down at Halford as the man struggled to get up again. He raised the gun and took careful aim.

Then he felt the cold barrel of another gun press sharply into his neck.

"I'll take that, if you don't mind," John Chance told him. "The party's over."

Chuck White hurried to the President. "Are you all right, sir?"

The President nodded. "Never mind me. What about everyone else? Have they freed the hostages?"

Marcie raised her gun. The two men with her mirrored the action.

"It's over," she said, aiming straight at the two Chinese men. "Let's do it."

On the floor in front of them, the hostages stared back, eyes wide and frightened. The Secret Service agents braced themselves for what they knew would be a suicidal attempt to reach the gunmen before they fired.

The gunmen were standing halfway between the two doors into the room, with a good view of both. So as soon as one of the doors was slammed open, all three of them turned and fired.

At empty space.

A second later, the other door crashed open. Dark shapes were silhouetted against the corridor outside. Red flashes filled the doorway. Three bodies dropped to the ground.

"Vulture One – three gunmen down. The eggs are safe. I repeat, the eggs are safe."

It seemed like everything was happening at once. Rich and Jade watched it all play out on the screens in the Surveillance Room. They saw Kate, Al and Barney speak briefly to three SAS soldiers, before kicking open the door to the room where the hostages were being kept and jumping back out of the way. A moment later, the soldiers booted open the other door and opened fire.

It was like they were watching a drama unfold on

television. But unlike television, they knew it was for real – it was happening all around them. They could hear the explosions and the gunfire. They could smell the cordite. They knew everyone that they could see was real.

Jade kept up a constant description of what was happening. There was no time for feedback from Roberts as he passed information to the soldiers who needed it, so Jade had no idea if she was helping or not.

The entire attack took less than three minutes, but by the end of it Jade was exhausted. She slumped back in her chair. Then Rich's words brought her suddenly back upright.

"Look – that's Kent. Coming this way."

Even as he said it, they heard the man clattering down the stairs above their heads.

"Kent's making for the Situation Room. For the President."

"Are Chance and White still in there?" Roberts asked immediately.

"They are."

There was the slightest pause. "Let's hope they see him coming. We have no radio contact with them."

On the screen, Kent was walking slowly but deliberately along the corridor, his gun raised.

Until someone brought bolt cutters or found a key for the handcuffs, the only way to free the President was to take the table apart. Chuck lay underneath it, using his pocket knife as a screwdriver as he tried to remove the bracing strut. The President was leaning down and offering advice, which Chuck accepted over-patiently.

Halford had managed to slide the handcuffs off his false leg and was strapping it back on. Chance's attention was all on Marshal Wieng who was sitting at the table with his hands on his head. Even though the Wieng tried to keep his expression neutral, Chance could tell he had seen something behind him.

Keeping the gun aimed at Wieng, Chance glanced back over his shoulder – and saw Kent standing in the doorway, his own gun levelled.

"Looks like we've got ourselves a standoff," Kent rasped. "Or have I been misinformed?"

But then he was suddenly propelled into the room, stumbling forwards as something hit him hard in the back. Halford grabbed Kent's gun as he went past, wrenching it free from the man's grip. Kent gave a shriek of agony as his bad arm hit the table, and he slumped to the floor.

"You've been misinformed," said Rich from the doorway.

"Doubly misinformed," said Jade, grinning beside her brother.

"Good to see you both," their father replied with a wry smile. "What kept you?"

"Watching telly," said Rich. "It had a happy ending."

Chance hauled Kent round the table and sat him next to Wieng. "I'm pleased to hear that. You done yet, Chuck?"

Chuck appeared from under the table, and the President stood up, stretching his legs. A handcuff dangled freely from one ankle.

"Despite the distractions," said Chuck, "yes, I'm done." He turned to the main control panel at the end of the room. "I'll just switch off the lock-down and the doors will unseal so we can get out of here."

"That will be a relief," said Chance. "You have a nice house, Mr President, but I shan't be sorry to leave it."

"Could do with redecorating," said Rich.

All around the White House, doors unlocked and windows unsealed. The Secret Service agents behind the heavy metal door that connected the West Wing to the main Mansion House heard the automatic bolts click undone. They pushed the door open.

In a sealed room hidden off the Chief of Staff's office, another door clicked. Even the badly damaged lock was cancelled as the lock-down was cancelled.

With a smile of satisfaction, Colonel Shu opened the door. She had heard the muffled sounds of the battle, and had no illusions about what must have happened. Even from the office, she could see the bodies of two of Kent's people lying in the corridor outside. She moved rapidly to collect the machine pistol one of them had dropped.

27

Smoke drifted along the corridors. They picked their way through debris and rubble, even stepping over bodies. Rich tried not to look too closely where he was putting his feet.

Dad had Marshal Wieng at gunpoint, while Chuck had his gun covering Jefferson Kent.

"I'm afraid you're not seeing my house at its best," the President admitted, following behind with Rich, Jade and Halford. Chuck had finally managed to get the handcuff off his ankle.

"Quite a party though," said Rich.

"Party's over," Chance told him.

"It's the morning after," Jade agreed. "Clear-up time."

"Talking of which," said Chance quietly as several

people appeared out of the misty air.

A number of SAS men in their black uniforms passed them, giving a thumbs-up and slapping Chance on the shoulder. But the three men now standing in the corridor had not taken a direct role in the raid.

Two were in army uniform, the stars on their uniforms marking their high rank. One of them looked distinctly sour. Behind them a man in an expensive dark suit seemed to be making a deliberate effort to keep in the background.

"General Sanchez," said the President. "Good of you to join us." He leaned to one side to get a better view of the man in the suit. "Oh, it's you. I take it I have you to thank for the damage to my wallpaper."

"Indeed, Mr President."

The sour-looking man saluted stiffly. "General Wilson, sir."

"General Wilson has come to tender his apologies. And, more importantly, his resignation," Sanchez said.

Wilson stepped forward, raising his hand, as if to shake the President's. But as it came up, Rich saw that the man was holding a pistol.

"Gun!" Chuck White yelled, launching himself at Wilson.

Chance also grabbed Wilson. Seeing his opportunity, Marshal Wieng turned to run.

But the man in the suit was standing in his way. "I don't think so," he said quietly.

Kent too was making a break for it – the other way back down the corridor. He dodged round Jade and ran straight at Rich.

Rich didn't move. He braced himself to try to stop the man. Then suddenly, Kent was falling. Behind Kent, Rich could see Jade's leg sticking out – she had tripped him as he dodged past. Kent crashed to the ground. His head hit the floor, and he lay still.

Halford was covering Wieng now as Chuck held General Wilson tight.

"Why?" the President asked.

"You should have brought them home," Wilson said. The contempt was obvious in his tone. "Those airmen, they shouldn't be left to rot in a Chinese jail. You should have negotiated and brought them home."

Further down the corridor, Marshal Wieng laughed.

The President shook his head. "They're dead, General. The Chinese sent two delegates to brief me yesterday, just before all this happened. They asked us not to announce it until they have the murderers in custody, though we've hardly had a chance anyway. The airmen were captured and executed as soon as they landed."

"Then you should have declared war!" Wilson spat.

"On China? General Wilson, those men were murdered by the rebels in Wiengwei," said the President. "The rebels who shot down their plane. On the direct orders of Marshal Wieng himself."

Wilson froze. "You're lying."

The President shook his head. "Ask him yourself."

Wilson turned. He shook off Chuck's grasp and marched stiffly towards Wieng, ignoring Chuck's gun aimed right at him as the Secret Service agent watched his every move. "Is that true?" Wilson demanded. "Did you and Kent lie to me?"

Wieng's face was twisted into a grotesque smile. "Kent didn't know. I imagine he will be as outraged as you are."

Both Chuck and Chance seemed to know what Wilson was intending. They grabbed him as he hurled himself at Wieng, dragging him back.

"We'll send him back to China," the man in the suit said. "Don't worry; he'll get the justice he deserves."

There was something in the way the man said it that made Rich shiver. He turned to look at Jade, now standing beside him. But it was the figure in the corridor behind her that made him cry out in alarm.

The slim, black-clad shape of Colonel Shu was sprinting towards them, her long plait of hair swinging as she ran, her machine pistol spitting fire.

Rich pushed Jade to one side, diving away with a warning yell.

Chance and Chuck dragged General Wilson to the floor. Halford pushed Marshal Wieng into a doorway, holding a handgun at the man's throat. The man in the suit spun as a bullet caught him in the arm. General Sanchez was hit in the leg and collapsed with a cry.

In the middle of it all, the President turned to face Colonel Shu. She was standing in front of him, legs apart as she braced herself from the recoil.

Rich threw himself at her from one side, Jade from the other. But Colonel Shu had already fired.

The man in front of her was caught full in the blast of gunfire and thrown backwards into the wall.

A split-second later both Rich and Jade hammered into Shu. Jade's rolling body knocked her legs away, as Rich crashed into her chest and sent her flying. But she kept hold of the gun. She rolled as she landed, like a paratrooper, and came up with the gun aimed right at Rich's head.

A single shot. A circle of red in the middle of the pale forehead.

Then Colonel Shu was falling to the ground. Behind her, Kate Hunter lowered her handgun.

The President looked up from the body of the man who had hurled himself in front of Colonel Shu's bullets. He shook his head. General Wilson was dead.

The President was making phone calls from the conference area at the end of the mobile headquarters truck. Rich and Jade sat with their dad, Halford, Chuck and Kate. Ardman was on his cell phone, sounding increasingly agitated, and Captain Roberts was massaging the top of his wounded leg.

"I think General Sanchez is next in line for that wheelchair," Chance told him.

"You don't need your leg anyway," said Halford. "You can manage without."

"I bet you miss yours," said Jade.

Halford nodded. "I do. I can still wiggle my toes though. Weird, isn't it. Sometimes my leg itches. It isn't there, but it itches. And I can't scratch it. How's that work?"

Ardman had finished on the phone. "Talking of itches

you can't scratch," he said, "I've just been talking to Goddard in London. Apparently our friend Ralph has regained consciousness."

"That's great," said Rich. "How is he doing?"

"Well, unfortunately no one seems to know. Goddard went to the hospital, but when the police on guard let him in to see Ralph, it wasn't him."

"What do you mean, it wasn't him?" said Jade.

"It was a Mr Mellor who's recovering from a car accident. They seem to think Ralph was transferred to another room. But that room is empty and there's no record he was ever there."

Chance laughed. "That sounds like Ralph."

"Pity though," Ardman went on. "I'd have liked to have thanked him for his help. As well as have a little chat about a few other matters."

"I think I know why he left," said Jade. "Before the fireworks."

"Talking of fireworks," said Rich to Chuck, "what's the deal with the Football then?" He lowered his voice. "I mean, was it really just a satellite phone all the time?"

"Not all the time," said Chuck. "Back in the sixties it was a proper launch facility like everyone thinks. But these days it's all a bit different."

"You don't need a big metal briefcase now," Kate told them. "This is the era of miniaturisation and global communications. The briefcase is a blind – a decoy if you like. The President doesn't need anything that clumsy and bulky to authorise a nuclear attack."

"Hell, these days," said Chuck, "you could do it with something like, I don't know, a modified cell phone. Speaking of which," he said to Jade, "you left Steve's phone in the Surveillance Room. But don't worry," he patted his jacket pocket. "It's safe enough now. And Steve's making a good recovery even after being shot by Rich here, so he'll look after it for the President again soon."

"Wait…" said Rich. "You mean, that phone was the nuclear launch device? All along?" He felt slightly faint at the idea that he had carried it in his pocket.

Chuck smiled. "Nowadays, all it takes is a phone call."

"I guess I have a lot of thanks yous to say, and I guess this is the place to start." The President was standing behind them. He looked tired, but confident as he shook hands with each of them in turn.

"That's quite a family you have there, Mr Chance," said the President.

"Don't I know it."

"One day we must meet without bullets flying and bombs going off in the background."

"That'd be nice," said Jade. "Mr President, sir," she added.

"I thought it was a great party, sir," Rich told him.

The President smiled. "You'll forgive me, but after being held hostage and threatened by madmen, I never want to go through anything like that again."

John Chance put a proud arm round his daughter's shoulder and patted his son on the back. "You said that last time, Mr President."

Although he smiled as he said it, only the President knew for sure if he was joking.

FIRST STRIKE